Seth and Mattie's Big River Adventure

story by
Sara Owen

---

story illustrations by
Rachel Renne & Heidi Anderson

scientific illustrations by
Terri Moore

D1365289

ISBN: 978-1-59152-236-2

Published by Sara Owen
© 2020 by Sara Owen
Story illustrations by Rachel Renne and Heidi Anderson
Scientific illustrations by Terri Moore

For more information contact:
Sara Owen, PO Box 1972, Helena, MT 59624
EMAIL: sethandmattieadventures@gmail.com
INSTAGRAM: @thenomadicecologist

sweetgrassbooks
an imprint of Farcountry Press

Produced by Sweetgrass Books; PO Box 5630, Helena, MT 59604;
(800) 821-3874; www.sweetgrassbooks.com.

Produced and printed in the United States of America.

23 22 21 20   1 2 3 4

For Mike

Who introduced me to the world of stream ecology

and

For Norb

Who always believed in this book.

Table of Contents

-1-

The River

Skim. . . . skim. . . . skim. . . . skim. . . . skim. . . . skimskimskimskim. . . . Seth watched the rock skip nearly all the way across the large pool. "Nine," he grumbled to himself. "I can do better." He picked up another flat, smooth, oval rock and sent it skimming over the water, snapping his wrist as he released the rock. That was the secret to good rock skipping—it was all in the wrist. His dad had taught him that when he was only eight years old. Now, at ten, Seth could outskip his dad. Seth's record was 12 skips, one better than his dad's best of 11. Skim. . . . skim. . . . skim. . . . skim. . . . Seth bit his lip—would it make it? . . . skim . . . skimskimskim . . . . Fourteen skips! *And the new rock-skipping champion of Newton County—with a new record 14 skips—is Seth Walker!" Seth raised his arms over his head and the crowd went wild.*

Seth's eyes refocused and he remembered he was standing alone on the gravel bar at the river. Some day it wouldn't just be a dream. For now, Seth decided to call it a day. Why not end on a good note? He couldn't wait to tell his dad about his new record.

Tired now, Seth climbed onto a large, flat rock in the middle of the river. It was his favorite rock in the entire river. It sat at the base of a 300 foot cliff, from which it had fallen millions of years ago. Over many eons, floods had smoothed its surface so that when Seth lay on his back, the rock was almost perfectly sculpted to him. Seth spent countless hours on this rock, sunning himself like a turtle and watching cumulus clouds float by in the sky, making silly shapes from them—a dancing bear, a mouse eating an ice cream cone, even a witch riding a broom, or was that his homeroom teacher, Mrs. Farnsworth? Seth laughed to himself. When the sun got too hot, he slithered into the cool water for a swim and chased the fish. FISH! Seth and his dad were supposed to go fishing tomorrow! Seth almost forgot! He ran home as fast as he could.

"Dad! Dad!" Seth burst through the back door and skidded into the kitchen. Seth's father looked up from the tomato he was slicing. "What is it, Seth?"

Panting hard Seth managed to get out, "We're still go-ing . . ." he caught his breath, "fishing tomorrow, right?"

"Did you *run* all the way home from the river?" his father asked. Still panting hard, Seth clutched his side and uttered an "uh-huh," then he collapsed into a heap on the floor, exhausted from his run. "Well," Seth's dad paused, "I think I have to work tomorrow," he teased.

"WHAT?" Seth jumped up. "But you *promised*!"

Seth's father laughed. "I'm only kidding, Seth. Of course we're still going fishing tomorrow. Remember, we have to get up very early."

"I don't care," Seth replied, his eyes gleaming. He was going to catch a big fish tomorrow, he just knew it. He'd been waiting for two weeks for the chance to fish with his dad again. "Oh, I almost forgot!" Seth blurted out. "I have a new rock-skipping record—fourteen!"

"Fourteen!" his father replied in astonishment. "Wow, Seth. You are really becoming quite the rock skipping pro. You should enter the rock skipping contest at the county fair this year."

The county fair? Seth's eyes glazed over as the sounds of cheering people filled his ears and images of a first-place trophy filled his head.

-2-

The Fishing Trip

Cock-a-doodle-doo! Cock-a-doo—Seth slapped his alarm clock. He hated the rooster alarm clock his Aunt Marcy got him for Christmas last year. He rolled over and looked out the window. It was still dark outside. He groaned and buried his head under the covers. Seth's father peeked into the room. He could see that Seth was going to need a little help getting out of bed, so he put on his fishing hat, slung his fishing rod over his shoulder, and marched into the room, chanting:

"I've got my line, I got my hook;
glance in the river—oh my! Look!
To my amazement I've just seen
a smallmouth bass staring back at me!

So bait the hook and off we go,
to fish and fish 'til the sun sets low.
Clean our catch and pack on ice,
mmm . . . hmmm . . . we'll eat well tonight!

BUT!" his father boomed, as he shook Seth's covers, "Only if you get . . . out . . . of . . . bed!"

"Okay, okay, I'm up!" Seth pleaded just as his father dragged the covers completely off the bed, revealing Seth's green and brown camouflage underwear. Seth jumped out of bed. "*DAD*! I said I was *up*!"

Seth's father grinned. "I was just making sure. Meet me downstairs in 10 minutes."

Seth struggled to pull his head through his shirt. "I bet I can make it in nine minutes," he challenged as his head popped through, his hair sticking on end from static electricity.

"Okay, nine minutes. And don't forget to brush your hair," his father laughed as he left the room. Seth looked in the mirror to see every strand of hair on his head sticking straight up in the air. *Definitely a hat day*, he thought, grabbing his fishing hat.

Eight and a half minutes later, Seth came barreling down the stairs, nearly tripping over the dog, Llama, who was asleep at the foot of the stairs. "Whoa, Llama! I didn't see you!" The shaggy sheepdog merely raised an eyebrow, then returned to his slumber. Seth ran to the back porch, where his dad was waiting, fishing rods and tackle box in hand. "See?" he boasted, pointing to his watch, "Less than nine minutes!"

"Very impressive," his father replied. "And with four whole seconds to spare. Are you ready?"

"YES! YES! YES!" Seth yelled, jumping up and down. And with that, Seth and his father headed down the path to the river.

There was evidence of daybreak on the horizon. The soft gray sky gave way to the slightest hint of yellow, which blended to a soft salmon, then to brilliant orange near the horizon. The air was so thick Seth could taste it—he could tell it was going to be a hot day. Birds were singing in the trees above—robins, cardinals, and blue jays. A pair of mourning doves stirred in the leaves, looking for an early morning meal. Droplets of dew covered the grass. As Seth and his father walked down the path, their feet brushed against the grass and soon their shoes and cuffs of their pants were soaked with moisture. Not that it mattered to Seth—he always took his shoes off at the river. By the time Seth and his father reached the river, the sun was beginning to peak above the horizon. The high bluff shaded the river well through the mid-morning, which worked in their favor. Not only would Seth and his father stay cool, but the fish would, too. Seth's father had explained to him that the fish like cool, shady water.

Once the sun was overhead, the water warmed up and the fish hid in shady, protected spots—where a fish hook couldn't reach. So the longer the sun stayed behind the bluff, the longer Seth could fish, and the better his chances of catching a big fish!

At the water's edge, Seth could see mosquito fish swimming in several schools, darting this way and that. He took his shoes off and threw them out of the way. He dipped his toe in the edge of the water and quickly pulled it back. "*Brrrr*! It's COLD!" Seth muttered. He grabbed his fishing rod and peeked into the tackle box. What sort of lure would they use today?

"Here, Seth," his father said as he pulled a lure with bright green rubber strands hanging from it, like a hula skirt. "Try this jig for the smallmouth bass." His father showed him how to attach the lure to the line. "Remember what we practiced last time? When you cast your line, make sure your arm points to where you want the lure to land. Right before your lure hits the water, give a little tug on your rod to help it land softly."

Seth nodded his head and cast his line onto the water. Immediately he felt a tug. "I got something!" he yelled to his father. His father watched as Seth tugged the line with little success. "This must be a BIG one!" he said, his brow furrowed in concentration.

"Do you need any help?" his father asked.

"No!" Seth asserted. "I got it." He was using his entire weight to pull the line, but it would not give. Beads of sweat lined his forehead. Frustrated, he gave one last yank and the line gave way. He stumbled backwards, tripped over a log, and landed flat on his rear end. His line flew out of the water, and caught in the hook was a tree branch!

His father burst out laughing. "That branch sure did put up a fight!" he teased. A look of disappointment crossed Seth's face. A stupid tree branch! How could he have been fooled by a stupid branch? Seth felt a tear come to his eye and quickly turned his head and wiped it away so his father wouldn't see. Seth's father saw the look on his son's face and quickly stopped laughing. "Did you hurt yourself?" he asked.

"No, but I don't think I want to fish anymore," he told his dad.

"Oh, come on, Seth. It's okay," he reassured him. He helped Seth up and brushed the dirt off of him. "I'll help you untangle your line and we'll try again." His father retrieved the branch from the edge of the river. Suddenly he saw something interesting on the limb. "Hey Seth! Look at this!"

"What is it?" Seth asked, confused.

"This branch has a colony of bryozoans* living on it," his father replied.

"Brian-what?" Seth asked.

"Bryo*zoans*," his father repeated. "Bryozoans are little animals that live in the water.

"Animals?!" Seth said in disbelief. "That just looks like a bunch of slime on a stick."

His father laughed. "Yes, it does," he said. "But there really are animals in all this slime. The animals themselves are cylindrical in shape with a large U-shaped crown of tentacles around their head. They use the tentacles to sweep water toward their mouths, then filter food from the water. They're also surrounded by a large mass of gelatin, which protects them. That's the slime you see. They're invertebrates, so they don't have a backbone like you and me. These animals are very tiny, so you have to look at them through a microscope. There are hundreds, maybe even thousands, of individual animals living on this stick."

*Pronounced: *"bry-oh-ZOH-enz"*

"Hmm . . . that's weird," Seth muttered. He wasn't sure what to think about these strange creatures. Then Seth spotted something crawling around on the limb. "Ooh! What's that?" he asked.

"An insect," his father replied. "See? It has six legs. That's how you know it's an insect." Seth stuck his nose right up to the limb to count the insect's legs. Sure enough, there were six legs. His father took a closer look.

"Hey, whadaya know? It's a dragonfly."

"What?" Seth exclaimed. "Dad, dragonflies live in the air, not the water. That thing looks like it should live in outer space."

"You're right, Seth, but not about the outer space part. Adult dragonflies do live in the air, but young dragonflies, like this one, live in the water. We call young dragon- flies nymphs.* Dragonfly nymphs are really neat—look at this." He pulled the dragonfly off the twig and, using his fingernail, gently pulled the lower lip of the dragon- fly away from its mouth and let it snap back. Seth's eyes widened.

"Whoa! What was that?" he asked excitedly.

"That," his father answered, "was the dragonfly's lower lip. Their lower lip looks like a mask that covers most of their face. Like this." He rested the heel of his

*Pronounced: *"nimfs"*

16

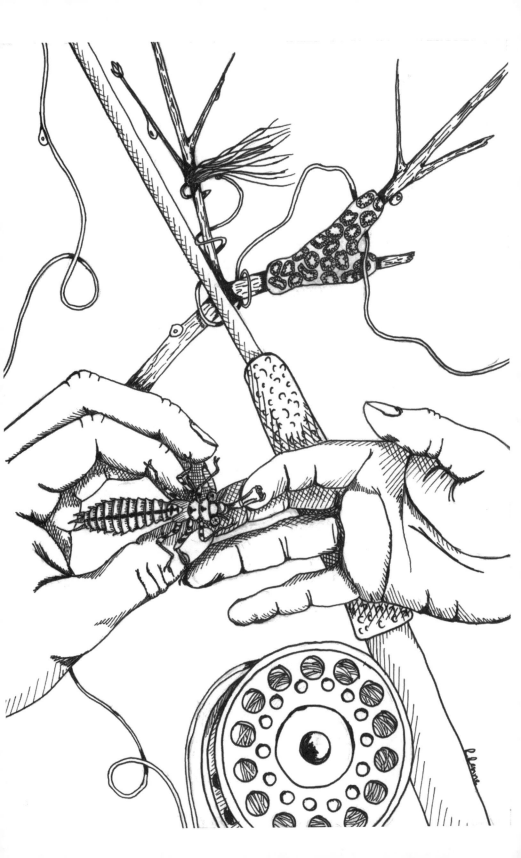

hand on his chin and cupped his fingers over the lower half of his face. "Dragonflies are predators," he continued, "so they catch live food. And they do that by extending their lower lip and grabbing their prey." He demonstrated by extending his arm toward Seth's face and grabbing his chin.

Seth was impressed. "Wow! That's really cool!"

"Yes, dragonflies are cool," his father replied. "There are many other kinds of insects and invertebrates that live in this river besides dragonflies and bryozoans."

"Really?" Seth asked. "Where do they live?"

"Well, most live between the rocks on the bottom of the river," his father explained. "Next time you're down here, turn over some rocks and see what you find." Seth's father untangled the fishing line from the branch. "You know, Seth, this was a rare find. Not many people get to see what we just saw. Good job, son." He tossed the stick back in the water and handed Seth's rod back to him. "How about we try this again?" he asked.

Seth smiled and nodded. His spirit for fishing had returned. "I'm gonna catch a *fish* this time," he promised.

They fished all morning and caught several fish. But the prize catch belonged to Seth—a two-pound smallmouth bass. Seth was so excited with his catch that afterwards he couldn't hold his rod still long enough for another fish to bite. He just kept glancing over at the bucket where they had put the "keepers." Every time he saw his fish swim by in the bucket, he broke into a grin. His father could tell their best fishing hours were behind them.

"Are you ready to go home and show Mom your catch?"

"Yeah," Seth answered. "I don't think I'm going to catch any more big fish today." A sly smile crept over his face. "They must have seen how I caught that other one, and now they're running scared!"

His father smiled. "Don't you mean 'swimming' scared?"

Seth laughed. "Yeah, I guess you're right." They packed up their gear, grabbed the bucket of fish, and headed home. Seth could hardly wait to show his mom the fish he'd caught.

-3-

Mattie

The next morning, Seth decided to go back to the river and look for more insects. He had been thinking about the dragonfly he found the previous day and was curious to see what other kinds of insects lived in the river. When he got to the water's edge, he tossed his tennis shoes on the shore, rolled up his pants, and slowly waded into the riffle. The water was so chilly he felt goose bumps pop up on his legs. He was glad the water in the riffle was shallow. It made getting used to the cold water easier.

Once he got used to the water's temperature, he began turning over rocks. The first rock he turned over had a bit of green algae* on the top—the bottom had nothing on it but slime. The next rock he turned over had something round and flat stuck to the bottom, but it wasn't moving so Seth didn't think much of it. Underneath the next rock he picked up, Seth saw a strange, tiny critter scurry away. It was very flat and it had a tail—*three* tails, to be exact. He noticed that the creature followed the water pooling on the rock and moved to shallow

*Pronounced: "AL-jee"

depressions that held small pockets of water. Seth stuck the rock right under his nose to get a closer look at this strange creature he'd discovered. Seth saw ripples moving down the critter's back. But as soon as the water drained off of the rock, the fluttering motion stopped. He wondered what caused the ripples to happen. Then Seth heard a voice.

"Hey! I'm dying down here!" it said.

Seth looked around, startled. "Huh? Who said that?" he asked.

"I did," the voice replied. "Down here, on the rock." Seth looked down and realized that it was the *creature* talking! "Quick!" the critter said, "I need to be in the water or I'll die!"

Seth gasped. *DIE!* he thought. He was so shocked that he panicked and dropped the rock without thinking. He watched in horror as the rock plunged into the river, splashing water all over him. *OH NO!* Seth thought. The fall surely killed the little creature. Suddenly he felt a sick feeling in his stomach. He wasn't sure what to do next. His first instinct was to run, but he knew deep down that wasn't the right thing to do. He also knew that if he didn't check on the little critter then it would bother

him the rest of the day. He took a deep breath, picked up the rock, and prepared himself to see the worst. When he turned it over he saw the little creature scurry for a shallow depression of water. Seth let out a sigh of relief.

"What *happened*?" the critter asked.

Seth paused. *Just tell it the rock slipped out of your hands*, he thought to himself. *It's just a little lie. How will it ever know the truth*? But Seth remembered what happened the last time he told a lie, and how upset and disappointed his mom was at him. He knew the right thing to do would be to tell the truth. "I panicked and dropped the rock," Seth said sheepishly. "I didn't mean to . . . it . . . it just happened. I'm really, really sorry."

"Well, in the future would you mind keeping the rock low to the ground and near the water? By the way, I'm Mattie. What's your name?"

"My name is Seth. It's nice to meet you, Mattie," he replied. Just then the water in the depression where Mattie was resting had nearly drained off the rock.

"Um . . . ." Mattie tapped his tails against the rock at the draining water. "Don't forget about the water."

"Oh! Right," Seth answered. He put the rock on the ground next to the river. He cupped his hands, dipped them into the river, and slowly poured water over the depression.

"Thanks," replied Mattie.

"So," Seth began hesitantly, "this may be a silly question, but what exactly *are* you?"

"I," Mattie stated proudly, "am a mayfly."

"Oh," Seth replied, confused. "What's a mayfly?"

"A mayfly is an insect," Mattie replied.

Seth took a closer look. "Oh!" he exclaimed. "Now I see your six legs!"

"Yeah," Mattie said. "All insects have six legs. How'd you know that?"

"My dad taught me that," Seth replied a little smugly. He felt very smart.

"Oh, so you think you know a lot about insects, do ya? Okay, smarty-pants, let's see if you know what else makes me an insect."

Seth thought back to the dragonfly he'd seen the day before. "Well, dragonflies can fly."

"Dragonfly!" Mattie screamed. "Where?! Help! Hide me, quick!" Seth watched as Mattie curled up into a trembling little ball.

"No, no! There's no dragonfly," Seth reassured him.

He laughed. "You're not an insect, you're a chicken."

"Ve-ry fun-ny," Mattie said haughtily. "I don't mess around with dragonflies. They eat mayflies like me."

"Oh yeah," Seth remembered. A devilish grin spread across his lips. "They're predators, so they grab their prey with their lower lip, like this." Seth covered his face with his hand and then reached out toward Mattie just like his father had shown him the day before.

"ACK! Cut it out!" Mattie said, waving his legs in front of his face. "You're scaring me, kid."

"Sorry," Seth said. Deep down he was still smiling. He knew he'd gotten the best of that little insect. "Okay, so back to your question. Insects can fly, right?" Then he remembered. "Oh wait! Ants can't fly, but they're insects, too, right?"

"That's right," Mattie said. "Can you think of something else that all insects have?"

"Hmm . . . well, when I step on bugs they usually go 'crunch!'" Seth said.

Mattie cringed. "Yeah, that's one way of putting it," he said. "That crunch is actually our skeleton, which we wear on the outside of our bodies. It's called an exoskeleton.* The exoskeleton prevents our bodies from losing

*Pronounced: "EX-oh-SKELL-uh-ton"

too much water. This isn't a problem for those of us that live in the river, but it's very important for ants and other insects to conserve water. The exoskeleton also protects us from scraping ourselves to pieces as we crawl around under the rocks, from hurting ourselves when we fight one another, and from getting *stepped* on . . . ." Mattie shot Seth a dirty look.

"Hey, I only step on cockroaches," Seth defended.

"The only bad thing about our exoskeleton," Mattie continued, "is that it prevents us from growing very much at one time."

"Does that mean you'll be this small forever?" Seth asked.

"No," Mattie replied. "Every few weeks we shed our exoskeleton so that we can grow. It's called molting."*

"What about being protected? What happens to you?" Seth asked.

"Well, our new exoskeleton will grow and harden very fast, but while we wait for it to harden, we have to find a place to hide so that we don't get hurt," Mattie answered.

"Whoa," Seth said, "that sounds scary."

"Normally it's not so bad," Mattie replied. "I usually

*Pronounced: *"MOHL-ting"*

hang out with a friend while I wait. But I remember one time after I molted when I was nearly swept downstream. I was snacking on some algae under a rock and I got a little too close to the main part of the river. I lost my hold on the rock, but luckily my cousin, Harry, was there and he grabbed one of my legs. I would've been okay, but he pulled so hard that he pulled my leg off. But I had—"

"What!" Seth interrupted. "He pulled your *leg* off?" You say it like it's no big deal! *Hello*? Didn't it *hurt*?" Then Seth looked closely at Mattie. Mattie had six legs. "Hey! You have all six of your legs! Are you making this up?"

"No, no, no!" Mattie insisted. "Let me explain . . . after I finish my story. Anyway, Harry pulled my leg off, but he stopped me long enough so I could get a good grip on the rock and crawl back to safety."

"Okay," Seth said, "so explain how you have six legs if your cousin pulled one off."

Mattie smiled. "Well, it just so happens that insects can grow back missing body parts."

Seth folded his arms across his chest. "I'm listening," he said skeptically.

"After we molt," Mattie began, "our exoskeleton is too big for us. This allows us to grow into it before we molt again. If we lose a leg, our body begins to grow a new one, except it can't be seen because it's under the exoskeleton. But when we molt again, our new leg appears, just like nothing ever happened."

"But doesn't it hurt to lose a leg?" Seth asked again.

"Sure, it stings for a little while. And once the leg starts growing back it gets a little cramped before we molt again. But it ain't so bad," Mattie replied. "I mean, at least I get my leg back eventually."

"Wow!" Seth said in awe. "That's so cool! Tell me more!"

Mattie thought for a second. "Okay. Insects also have unique eyes. We have what are called *compound* eyes. You humans only have two simple eyes, each with just one lens, but we have many lenses—hundreds or even thousands—in each of our two compound eyes, so they are very large and round."

"So, do you see hundreds of pictures of the same thing?" Seth asked.

"No, we see one picture, just like you, only ours is a little fuzzy. And you know what else? We can see behind us without turning our heads," Mattie said.

"No way!" Seth exclaimed.

"Yup, it's true," Mattie replied. It was his turn to feel smug.

Seth was amazed. "Wow. This is just so cool. Y'know, before yesterday I didn't know anything about insects. I especially didn't know you guys could live in the water." Then Seth realized something didn't make sense. "But how do you breathe in the water?" he asked.

"We have gills," Mattie answered.

"You mean like fish?" Seth asked.

"They are similar, yes, but fish gills are protected by a bony cover on their heads called an operculum.* Our gills are on our backs, and very vulnerable to being damaged."

The light bulb went off in Seth's head. His eyes widened and he gasped, "That's what I saw rippling down your back, wasn't it? Your gills!"

"Uh-huh," Mattie said. "That's why I needed to stay in the water. Our gills have to stay wet in order to work. If they dry out, we can't breathe." Seth suddenly became very conscious about keeping water on the rock for Mattie. He quickly poured more water on the rock, and kept pouring, and pouring. "Hey, Seth!" Mattie yelled. "It's not necessary to drown me!"

"Oh, sorry," Seth apologized. "I just wanted to make

*Pronounced: *"oh-PER-kyoo-lum"*

sure you didn't dry out. Can you really drown?"

"No, silly, I *live* in the water." Mattie laughed. "Gotcha!"

Seth realized what he had said. "Oh, man, you did get me."

"So Seth, would you like to meet more insects that live in the river?" Mattie asked.

"Really?" Seth asked excitedly. "I could do that?"

"Sure, c'mon. It'll be fun—there's a whole other world down there, Seth. So let's go!" Mattie said.

-4-

The Adventure Begins

Mattie noticed Seth was giving him a quirky look. "What's wrong?"

"Um, one problem," Seth said. "I'm a little too big to be crawling around under the rocks."

"Oh!" Mattie exclaimed. "My, my. Yes, you are too big aren't you?"

"Does this mean I don't get to go?" Seth asked disappointedly.

"Nah, I'll just have to fix things, that's all," Mattie replied. "You must follow these instructions exactly. Pick me up and hold me in the palm of you hand." Seth bent down and first put some water in his hand. "Good thinking," Mattie said. "Easy now. Watch the gills." Seth gently picked up Mattie and set him in his left hand. "Now, fold your fingers over and make a fist—but not too tight," Mattie instructed. Seth did as he was told, careful not to squish the little mayfly. "Now, close your eyes and count backwards from five."

Seth closed his eyes and began to count backwards. "Five . . . four . . . three . . . two . . . ONE." Seth felt something strange happen, like every cell in his body was shaking. He was dying to see what was going on, but he didn't dare open his eyes for fear of what might happen to him.

"You can open your eyes now," Mattie said. When Seth opened his eyes he was standing on a rock. When Seth looked over at his new friend, he gasped—Mattie was the same size Seth was! He breathed in a mouthful of water and immediately coughed, trying to get the water out of his lungs, but when he took another breath, it was more water. That's when Seth realized he was under water, and that Mattie wasn't the same size as he was, but that *he* was the same size as *Mattie*. Seth quickly held his breath and looked at Mattie for help. "It's okay," Mattie reassured him. "You can breathe normally."

Seth let out a mouthful of air bubbles and a sigh of relief. "So I'm not going to drown?"

"I don't think so," Mattie teased. Seth's eyes widened. Mattie laughed. "You'll be fine, Seth. Trust me."

What have I gotten myself into? Seth wondered. *And why am I trusting this mayfly with my life? I mean, he's just an insect! How big can his brain be?* Seth took a deep breath. There was nothing he could do now but trust Mattie and hope for the best. He looked around to get a better sense of his surroundings. The rock he was standing on was in a little trench, out of the main current of the river. There were large rocks all around, with very dark areas underneath them. Seth didn't like the looks of those dark areas. Mattie saw the concerned look on Seth's face. "C'mon, that's where we're going," he said.

"What?! Are you serious?" Seth asked. "I'm not going down *there*. How do you know there isn't something down there waiting to eat you?"

"That's where I live. That's how I know," Mattie replied.

"Oh," Seth said. He still didn't like the idea of crawling into a dark hole.

Mattie noticed Seth still wasn't convinced. "It's okay, I promise. Just stick close to me and everything will be fine."

"It's not that I'm afraid to go with you, but . . ." Seth hesitated, "I'm afraid of the dark," he said quietly.

"Hmmm…" Mattie thought about the situation for a minute, then he had a brilliant idea.

"Don't worry, Seth. Give me a few minutes and everything will be okay." Mattie swam over to the water's edge, stuck his head out of the water and yelled something Seth couldn't hear. "Everything is taken care of," he said when he returned.

"What did you do?" Seth asked.

"I called upon my friends, the glow worms, who will light our path so you won't be afraid," Mattie replied.

"Glow worms?" Seth asked. "What are those?"

"Glow worms are insects that can emit light from their bodies by a process called bioluminescence.* They're related to fireflies," Mattie answered.

"Oh, you mean lightening bugs? I like lightning bugs," Seth said.

Mattie nodded. "Yep, same thing. Glow worms aren't truly aquatic, so they don't actually live in the river, but along the shore. They can't light our entire path, but they can light it for a short way, at least until you get used to the dark. Your eyes will adjust to the darkness over time, and soon you'll be able to see just fine."

This eased Seth's mind somewhat. He made up his mind right there that he was not going to be the chicken. He would look at the situation as a great adventure, going where no human had gone before. Like Marco Polo, Ferdinand Magellan, and Sir Edmond Hillary, Seth Walker would join the ranks of the great explorers of the world.

Mattie tapped Seth on the shoulder. "Look," he said, pointing up. Seth looked up to see a herd of glow worms

*Pronounced: *"BYE-oh-loom-uh-NESS-ens"*

crawling down the rock toward them. The glow worms lined up over the dark canyon Seth and Mattie would soon be entering. Each glowworm emitted a greenish light that cast an eerie glow into the dark hole. "Is that better?" Mattie asked.

"It's still a little scary, but at least I can see now," Seth replied.

"Are you ready?" Mattie asked.

"I guess so," Seth said.

"Here, you can hold my claw," Mattie said.

"Okay," Seth said, then hesitated.

"What's wrong?" Mattie asked.

"Which claw do I hold?" Seth asked.

"Huh, I hadn't thought about that. Which one would you like to hold?" Mattie asked.

"Well, I know I don't want to hold the one that your cousin ripped off," Seth answered. "It's already been jinxed."

"Okay," Mattie said. "Why don't you hold this one." He stuck out his front left leg for Seth. "Now are you ready?" Mattie asked.

Seth took a deep breath. "I'm as ready as I'll ever be," he said.

-5-

Penny

Mattie and Seth slowly swam into the dark hole. With the glow worms lighting the way, Seth could see weird-looking creatures crawling around on the sides of the rocks and among the pebbles below them. Seth moved closer to Mattie. "It's okay," Mattie said. "We're completely safe. All of these guys are friendly. Just then they passed the last glow worm, and Seth watched it crawl back to the shore, back to the safe, bright daylight. He turned his attention back to the water and realized that Mattie had been right—his eyes had adjusted to the darkness.

"Wanna meet my cousin?" Mattie asked.

"Sure. Is this the same one who pulled off your leg?" Seth asked.

"Yup," Mattie replied.

"And you still talk to him?" Seth asked in disbelief.

"Of course I still talk to him. It was an accident. Forgive and forget. And besides, it *grew back*," Mattie reminded Seth. He crawled under a rock and motioned for Seth to follow. "Down here."

"Mattie, I can't crawl on the under side of the rock. I don't have claws like you."

"Just try it," Mattie called out in a muffled voice.

"Okay," Seth sighed. *Well, at least I'm in the water so when I fall off this rock, the water will cushion my fall*, he thought to himself. Seth grabbed onto the rock and swung his feet up onto it but he *didn't fall!* "Hey! Check this out! I'm hanging onto the rock up-side-down!" Seth crawled after Mattie, over the bumps and depressions in the rock. Seth climbed up onto a small mound and paused. Suddenly he felt the mound move! "MATTIE!" Seth called out. "Mattie! The rock is moving!" Mattie turned around to see what the fuss was about. He began laughing and swam back to Seth.

"That isn't the rock! That's a beetle!"

"Where's a beetle?" Seth asked quizzically. It seemed like nothing this mayfly said ever made sense.

"Underneath you. The thing you felt move," Mattie replied.

"I've seen beetles before, and I know that's no beetle," Seth said. "Where's its head?"

"Well, you've already noticed . . . well, actually you *didn't* notice, that this beetle looks like the rock." Mattie tapped on the beetle's back. "It is very flattened and has these overlapping plates that protect it and help disguise it. Let's see who's home." Mattie lifted up the flap near the front end of the beetle. "Ah, here's its head," Mattie said. "Take a look."

Seth leaned over to take a peek, but instead bumped his head on the rock below. "Ow!" he cried.

"Maybe you should climb down here and take a look," Mattie advised.

"Thanks for the tip," Seth replied sarcastically. He let go of the rock and did a backward flip as he floated down to Mattie.

"Take a peek, show-off," Mattie said. Seth peered under the flap Mattie was holding up.

"Hey! There's his head!" Seth said.

"Yeah, I just said that," Mattie stated.

"He's really cute—he reminds me of a turtle! He has his very own shell that he lives under!" Seth said.

"But remember what I said? It's a beetle, which means it's an insect like—"

"Oh my gosh!" Seth exclaimed. "He moved again!" The beetle turned its head back and looked at Seth and Mattie.

"Just for the record," the beetle said in a dignified voice, "I'm a SHE." The beetle took a better look at Seth. "Oh, my! You're a human!" she said, startled.

"Is that a bad thing?" Seth asked.

"Oh, no," the beetle replied. "It's just I've just never seen one this close before," she answered.

"I'm sorry for calling you a boy," Seth said.

"It's quite alright. It's difficult to tell just by looking at my head. My name is Penny," the beetle said. "Sometimes you'll hear people call me a 'water penny.' That's how I got the name Penny. What's your name?"

"My name is Seth, and this is my friend, Mattie. He's a mayfly."

"It's nice to meet you both," Penny replied.

"Hmmmm. You look very familiar," Seth said, "but I'm not sure where I've seen you before. Maybe I'll remember later. How come you don't look like any beetle I've ever seen?" he asked.

"Probably because most beetles you see on land are adults. I'm not an adult yet. I'm still a larva. When I'm ready to become an adult, I'll build a pupa* and then undergo a metamorphosis,"** Penny answered. "When I become an adult, I'll live on the land."

*Pronounced: *"PYOO-puh"*
** Pronounced: *"met-uh-MORE-fuh-sis"*

"The pupa is like the cocoon a caterpillar builds when it becomes a butterfly," Mattie chimed in.

"Oh, so you're an insect?" Seth asked.

"Yes I am," Penny replied.

"I *just* said that!" Mattie exclaimed. "Do you *listen*?"

Seth ignored him. "Where are your legs?" he asked.

"They are hidden beneath these large plates on my back," she replied. "Hold on and I'll show you." Seth heard a soft 'pop' and watched as Penny floated down to him. She landed on her back and wiggled her legs in the water. "Here they are!"

"Wow! You really are like a turtle, completely covered by those large plates."

"The plates also act like a suction cup and hold me to the rock really tight," Penny said.

"Oh, *that's* what that popping noise was," Seth said. Suddenly he remembered where he'd seen Penny before. "I remember!" he shouted.

"What?" Penny and Mattie asked.

"I remember where I saw Penny. Earlier this morning—on the first rock I picked up! That was you!"

"I *thought* I felt a draft this morning," Penny mused.

Seth noticed Penny had frilly white things on her belly. "What are these?" he asked.

"Those are my gills," Penny explained.

Seth ran his hand over them. "They feel really soft."

Penny giggled. "That tickles!" Seth began running both hands over her gills. "Whoa, whoa, that tickles!" she squealed. "St-st-stop! Hah, hah, that tickles!" Penny's legs were waving wildly in the air. "Hee hee hee! Oh my gosh, stop! STOP! That *tickles*!"

WHACK! One of Penny's legs hit Seth in the head and he went sailing backwards into the rock.

"Seth! Are you okay? Seth! Speak to me!" Mattie swam over to Seth and helped him up. As Seth began to walk, his legs were a little wobbly.

Penny regained control of herself. "Oh my gosh! Did I hurt you?"

Seth laughed. "No, I'm okay." He rubbed the spot on his head where Penny's leg hit him. "I don't even think it will form a knot. I'm glad I was underwater, though. It softens the blow much better than air."

"She nailed you good, Seth," Mattie said.

"I know. That's quite a kick you got there," Seth said. "I'd hate to see what you could do if you were mad."

Penny smiled. "That's not the first time I've heard that," she said.

"I hate to break up the party, but we really need to find my cousin. Do you feel okay to swim?" Mattie asked.

"Yeah, I feel fine," Seth answered.

"Before you leave, if it's not too much trouble, could you help me back up onto the rock?" Penny asked.

"Sure," Mattie answered. "Grab hold, Seth." Seth grabbed one side of Penny's back while Mattie grabbed the other. "On the count of three, okay?" Mattie said. Seth nodded. "One . . . two . . . THREE!" Seth and Mattie both flung their arms—and Penny—up into the water. Penny rushed toward the rock above, grabbed it with her claws, and pulled herself up.

Seth swam up to her and lifted her head flap. "Good-bye, Penny."

"Good-bye, Seth. It was nice to meet you." Seth released the flap and he and Mattie made their way out from under the rock into an area of open water.

-6-

Norris

A blur swam toward them, nearly running Seth over. "Hey!" Seth exclaimed. "What was that?"

"Oh! That's Harry! Wait here while I catch up with him and you can meet him," Mattie said.

"Wait! Don't leave me here by myself!" Seth exclaimed in terror.

"Don't worry! I won't be gone more than a couple of seconds," Mattie assured Seth. "Here, sit in this little cave so you'll be out of sight of any predators."

"Promise you'll be back soon?" Seth asked nervously. He did not like the thought of being abandoned in an unfamiliar place.

"Promise," Mattie said as he darted after his cousin.

Seth stood at the opening of the cave squinting, trying to see what, if anything, was in it. Darkness. He hoped nothing was back there because he wasn't interested in sharing his refuge with anybody. Cautiously Seth crawled back into the space, feeling his way around with his hands. He put his hand onto something slimy and cringed. Ew! he thought, yanking his hand back and waving it around in the water to wash the slime away. He knew there were a thousand possibilities as to what that slime could have been, but he didn't want to think about it. Seth turned around and sat down with his back against one of the side walls. That way he could see Mattie when he returned and he didn't have his back completely turned to the back of the cave. He wasn't sure if anything was back there, but he wasn't about to turn his back on the *possibility* that something was back there. That was a good way to get an unpleasant surprise, and Seth hated surprises. He sat there motionless, praying that Mattie would hurry back. It was creepy in the cave.

Seth felt something touch his foot, then slowly begin to wrap itself around his ankle. He jumped up and shook his foot, knocking the unknown creature off. He broke into a karate stance, ready to defend himself. *I am a ninja*, he told himself. His heart was racing.

"Who's there?" he asked assertively. A ghostly figure emerged from the darkness. It was slender and snaking its way toward him. Seth saw this as a great opportunity— to run. He scrambled out of the cave, his arms and legs flailing in every direction. He took off swimming wildly in the direction that Mattie had left just a minute earlier.

"Mattie! MATTIE!" Seth yelled. "Something tried to get me!" Mattie and his cousin, Harry, were on their way back to where he'd left Seth, when they heard Seth calling.

"Uh-oh," Mattie told his cousin. "Something has freaked Seth out. We'd better see what's wrong." They quickly made their way over to Seth. "What's up, Seth?" Mattie asked.

"S-s-something's in there and it tried to get me! It wrapped itself around my ankle, but I got away." Seth was trembling.

"What did it look like?" Mattie asked.

"It looked like a snake!" Seth answered.

"A snake?" Harry said. "If he saw a snake it would be absolutely huge."

"I don't know what it was, but I'm telling you, it was long and skinny and it looked like a *snake*!" Seth said.

"What color was it?" Mattie asked.

"It looked white."

"Hmmm…well, I guess we have to go see what it is," Mattie said.

"NO WAY am I going back in there!" Seth spat out.

"Okay, then you can wait here," Mattie replied.

"No! I don't want to be left alone again!"

"Alright then, I guess you're coming with us." Mattie stared at Seth.

"Fine," Seth grumbled.

"Heyyyyy," Harry said, "I bet I know what it was. I bet it's Norris."

"Ah, of course, a horsehair worm. I should have known," Mattie said.

"What's a horsehair worm?" Seth asked. Mattie followed Harry into the cave, but Seth hung around near the opening, unsure if he wanted to go in again. "What's a horsehair worm?" he asked again. Harry swam right to the back of the cave.

"Norris? Is that you?" he called into the darkness. There was a stir and then the ghostly figure that Seth had seen earlier made its way toward Harry.

"Who's calling?" the figure asked.

"Norris, it's Harry. I have a friend I want you to meet."

"Harry? Is that you? Come here, my boy. It's been a long time since I've seen you."

"Come on in, Seth, I want you to meet somebody," Harry said. Seth eased his way back to where Harry and Mattie were waiting, and again stuck his hand in the nasty slime. *Ughhhh, gross!* Seth shook his hand in annoyance. When he reached them, he saw the ghostly figure in its entirety.

"Seth," Mattie said, "this is a horsehair worm. Norris, I'd like to introduce you to my human friend, Seth."

"Come closer, boy, so I can get a better look at you," Norris replied.

"He's nearly blind, so you have to stand right next to him so he can see you," Mattie whispered to Seth. Seth moved closer.

"Hello, s-sir," he said shakily.

"My goodness. I've never seen a human in all my life," Norris said.

"It's nice to meet you, sir," Seth replied.

"I'm sorry to have scared the life out of you earlier," Norris chuckled. "I was looking for my spectacles. Can't see much of anything without my spectacles." Seth took a closer look at this strange worm. He was incredibly long and slender, like a snake, but he wasn't really like a snake, either. Seth didn't know what to make of him.

"Mattie, he doesn't have any legs," Seth whispered. "Are you sure he's not a snake?"

"I'm sure. Snakes have a backbone and are vertebrates,

like you. Norris is an invertebrate, so he doesn't have a backbone," Mattie answered. "He's a type of worm, similar to an earthworm, only without any segments. They are very simple organisms, with very tiny brains. But don't tell Norris that—he's actually a very wise horsehair worm. He's been alive longer than anybody else in the river. He has some really cool stories about when he was a little horsehair worm. Ask him about the story when his brothers were born!"

"Yeah, Norris, tell us about the birth of your younger brothers," Harry said. Seth was interested now, so he relaxed and settled down for the story.

"Well, when my younger brothers were born. . . ." Norris interrupted himself. "You boys don't really want to hear this story again, do you?"

"We love the story, and Seth hasn't heard it before," Mattie urged.

"I'd like to hear the story, if you don't mind, Norris," Seth said politely.

"Well, alright, then. Where was I? Ah, yes. When my younger brothers were born, they did not have working stomachs. In order to gain nutrients to grow, they moved into a grasshopper and got their nutrients from it. When they got big enough, they burst out of the grasshopper and joined the rest of the family in the river."

"EW!" Seth said in disgust. "What happened to the grasshopper?"

"Well, the grasshopper died," Norris answered. "That's just how it works, my boy."

"Norris and his brothers are parasitoids,"* Mattie explained, "which means he lived inside another organism and got his nutrients from it while he was a baby. As an adult, though, he can live on his own. But it's all at a cost to the host."

"That's gross, not to mention a mean thing to do to a grasshopper," Seth said.

"In my own defense," Norris began, "there are many other kinds of worms that live as parasites in humans, and they can make the humans very sick. But horsehair worms are not one of those worms."

Seth thought about this for a minute. It was kind of a neat thing, a grasshopper exploding with worms squirming out of its body. And it wasn't like there was a shortage of grasshoppers around. Seth's dad often complained about grasshoppers being pests that gobbled up the vegetables in their garden. Maybe horsehair worms

*Pronounced: *"pair-uh-SIT-oydz"*

helped reduce the number of grasshoppers. It could be worse, he thought. At least Norris wasn't a human parasite. He'd have to remember to tell his mom this story—it would really gross her out.

"Seth?" Mattie waved a hand in front of Seth's face. "Seth, you're spacing out. Are you okay? Are you going to be sick?"

"No, I'm cool with it," he replied. "I can't wait to tell my mom that story. It will totally gross her out!"

"Well, it looks like you've done your part to better the world, Norris," Harry said.

"I guess my work here is done," Norris answered. "Ah! Here are my spectacles!" The worm maneuvered the spectacles onto his head with his tail.

"We really should be on our way," Mattie said. "I'm taking Seth on a tour of the river, and we have a lot to see before the day is over."

"Have you taken him by Old Griswald's place yet?" Norris asked.

"Not yet," Mattie replied.

"Who?" Seth asked.

"Old Griswald is a water bear. You may get to see him later."

"Oh," Seth answered, confused. "Okay." *A bear?* Seth thought. He began to realize that there was nothing normal about any of the creatures that lived in this river.

"Well, Norris, I believe it is time for us to mosey on," Harry said.

"Just in time for my nap," Norris answered.

"Then we'll be on our way," Mattie said. "Thank you for sharing your story."

"I'm tickled you boys dropped by. It's nice to chat with you young folks every now and then. Drop by anytime," Norris said. "It was certainly nice to meet you, Seth."

"It was very nice to meet you, too," Seth said. "Thanks for the great story."

With that, Mattie, Harry, and Seth left Norris to his nap.

Harry

Back in the main river, Mattie suddenly realized something. "Oh my goodness! In all the commotion earlier, I never introduced the two of you! Seth, this is my cousin I was telling you about, Harry. Harry, this is Seth, the boy I met earlier this morning."

Seth had been studying Harry ever since he saw him. He looked a lot like Mattie, but there was something different about him. He had two large triangle-shaped flaps on his back. Mattie noticed Seth looking at them.

"Those are his gills. They are operculate,* meaning they cover some of the other gills.

"So that's what those things are. I'd been wondering about it the whole time," Seth said. Harry flapped his gills in the water so Seth could get a better look. "Wow! That's really cool!" Seth said.

"Yeah, the chicks dig 'em," Harry said.

Mattie rolled his eyes.

"So, how do you like the river?" Harry asked.

"It's definitely been exciting so far," Seth replied.

"There's never a dull moment down here," Harry said.

"I'm beginning to discover that for myself," said Seth.

*Pronounced: *"oh-PER-kyoo-lat"*

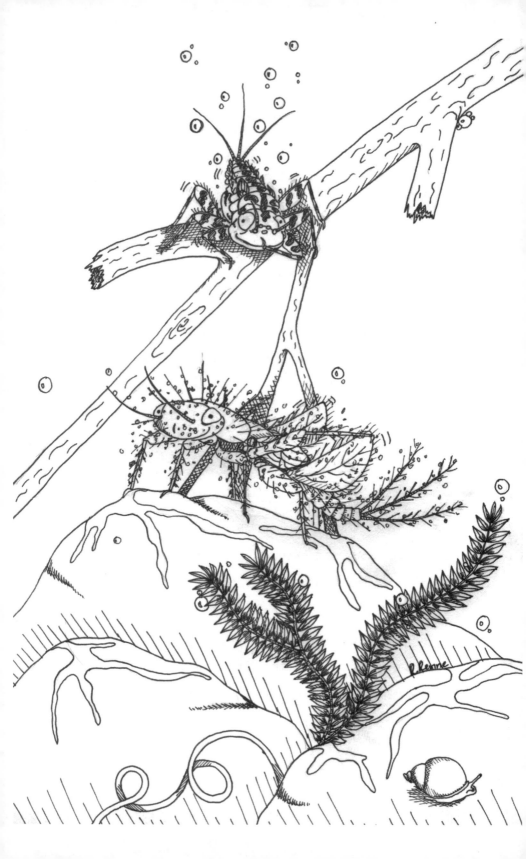

He had noticed something else strange about Harry while they had been talking with Norris—he was very . . . dirty. A cloud of debris surrounded him and followed him wherever he went. Before Seth could stop himself, he blurted out, "Why are you so dirty?" Seth immediately clamped his hand over his mouth.

"Seth!" Mattie scolded. "That was very rude."

"I'm so sorry, Harry. I didn't mean to say that."

"Don't sweat it, Seth," Harry replied. "I get that a lot. I look dirty because I have algae growing all over the long setae* on my legs and body."

"*Setae*? What's that?" Seth asked.

"Setae are stiff hairs that grow on our bodies. Most insects have at least some setae. I just happen to have much longer setae than most—and a lot more of them," Harry replied.

"Wait a minute. Did you say you have *algae* growing on you?" Seth asked again, just to make sure he heard Harry correctly.

"Yes I did," Harry answered.

"Ugh! Algae are gross and slimy. Doesn't your mom make you take a bath? My mom would kill me if I let something funky like that grow on me!" Seth exclaimed.

*Pronounced: *"SEE-tee"*

"Take a bath!" Harry cried. "Why no! The algae are a part of me, a part of the entire river. They are the base of the food web, producing a lot of the food that is eaten by invertebrates. Without the algae, we wouldn't be here because there would be nothing to eat. I'm proud to have algae living on me because I know that when I crawl under a rock and some of it scrapes off of me, some invertebrate downstream is going to eat that algae. I'm just doing my part to sustain a healthy river."

"But the real reason is because all the girls like the cute, furry look the algae give him," Mattie chimed in.

"Can I help it if I'm a ladies' mayfly?" Harry asked.

"Oh, brother," Seth said. It was Seth's turn to roll his eyes.

"What?" Harry asked. "You don't think it makes me look cute?"

"Well. . . ." Seth hesitated. He was kinda cute. "I guess so," he said. He was still a little weirded out by the whole idea of algae growing on his body. He leaned over to Mattie and whispered, "Remind me to thank my mom for making me take all those baths."

-8-

Old Griswald

"Oh man! I gotta get home! My mom's waiting on me," Harry realized.

"We'll walk with you part of the way. Let's go by Old Griswald's house and see if we can get a glimpse of him," Mattie said.

"Who is this Griswald guy?" Seth asked with a hint of irritation in his voice. No one would tell Seth anything about Old Griswald, and he was beginning to get annoyed.

"Old Griswald is an unusual invertebrate that lives in the river and he looks just like a bear. I thought you would like to see him," Mattie said.

"Can I meet him?" Seth asked.

"NO!" Harry said. "I've heard he eats small insects! He's got giant claws! And a big piercing mouth! He might try to eat us! Suck us dry!" Seth's eyes widened in terror.

"Harry! That's not true. Stop trying to scare Seth," Mattie scolded. "Seth, Old Griswald is not an insect eater. He does have four large claws on each of his eight legs, and he does have a big piercing mouth, but he does *not* eat insects." Mattie shot Harry a dirty look. "He drinks the juices out of plants and mosses. He is very reclusive, so nobody knows much about him. We'll be lucky to even see him. I don't even know anyone who has ever talked to him. He's very mysterious. But there's no reason to worry."

Seth relaxed. He was curious about this Old Griswald, and wanted to see what he looked like. The three of them crawled along the bottom of the riverbed, staying out of the main current so they wouldn't get swept downstream. Suddenly Mattie grabbed Seth's arm.

"There it is."

"What?" Seth asked.

"Old Griswald's home." Seth looked over at the edge of the river, up near the surface, and saw a large mass of moss growing on several large rocks. It was very dark and scary looking.

"That? He lives up there? No wonder everybody's scared of him. That whole place is scary."

"Wanna see if we can get a look at him?" Mattie asked.

"Yeah," Seth said. Being so small, he was worried about lurking predators, but his encounter with Norris made Seth as curious as he was anxious. Now he was intrigued and wanted to get a look at Old Griswald. They crawled down behind a rock where they couldn't be seen, but they could still see Old Griswald's home. "I want to get closer," Seth said.

"I don't think that is such a good idea, Seth," Mattie said.

"Why not? You said he doesn't eat insects." Seth said.

"Yeah, but he didn't say he doesn't eat humans," Harry teased.

"Harry!" Mattie scolded. "Seth, nobody knows anything about Old Griswald. He may have dragonflies guarding the place, or even something worse. And truthfully, I don't want to know."

"Okay, okay," Seth said disappointedly. He saw something move in the moss. "Look, the moss is moving! Is it him?" They got very quiet and concentrated on the moss. Then they saw a bearlike animal lumber out of the dark shadows, climbing around on the moss, apparently looking for something. "Whoaaaaa," Seth said under his breath. Now he understood why Mattie had called him a water bear. Old Griswald looked a lot like a bear, only he had eight legs and a long, pointy mouth.

"See his mouth?" Mattie asked. "That's what he uses

to drink juices from the plants. It's like a straw." Seth was mesmerized by the water bear. It was a very unique-looking creature, yet it was so beautiful.

"I think he's neat," Seth said. Then Old Griswald looked up, straight at Mattie, Harry, and Seth.

"He saw us!" Harry cried. "Quick, let's get out of here!" He and Mattie turned and swam away as fast as they could. But Seth stayed behind.

"Come on, Seth!" Mattie hissed.

Seth just stood there looking at Old Griswald. Old Griswald stared back, and their eyes locked. Seth waved and gave a little sideways grin. Old Griswald waved back, then crawled back into the shadows. Seth almost thought he saw Old Griswald return a smile. Old Griswald wasn't a threat to anyone, Seth thought to himself, he was just misunderstood. Old Griswald was probably very friendly, if others in the river would take the time to get to know him. Seth sighed and turned and swam away to catch up with Mattie and Harry.

-9-

The Mussel

"**W**hat were you thinking?" Harry yelled. "You could have gotten yourself killed— or worse!"

"I just waved at him, and he waved back," Seth replied defensively. "Maybe he's just lonely."

"Hmph," Harry muttered. "I still wouldn't talk to him for all the algae I could eat."

"That's enough," Mattie said firmly. "Harry, we're nearly at your house. I'm going to take Seth on down the river, but I'll be back at your house in time for supper."

"Okay," Harry said as he turned to leave. "Seth, I hope you enjoy the rest of your trip."

"Thanks, Harry. I've enjoyed it so far," Seth said.

"You guys be careful and watch out for dragonflies. We've been lucky so far," Harry warned.

"We'll be careful," Mattie said.

"Bye, Seth. See you around," Harry said.

"Bye. Nice to meet you, Harry." Seth waved as he and Mattie swam away. "Where to now?" he asked.

"I don't have any place in mind, so I thought we'd just

float downstream a ways and see what we can see. How does that sound?" Mattie proposed.

"Sounds good to me," Seth said. "I'm following you."

"Let's go," Mattie said as he led Seth down to the cracks between the rocks. "We'll stay down here so we won't get caught in the current. Bad things happen when you get caught in the current unexpectedly." Seth was careful to follow closely behind Mattie. Even though they were out of the main current, Seth could still feel a strong push from the water on his back.

"I don't see how you do this everyday. Don't you get tired of fighting the water current?"

"This is an unusual place for me to be," Mattie said. "Normally I'm underneath these rocks, completely out of the current, like Penny."

"Why are you up here, then?" Seth asked.

"Well, it's kind of hard to show you the river if you can't see it." Mattie stopped abruptly.

"What's wrong?" Seth asked.

"Nothing, I just found a new invertebrate to show you."

"Where?" Seth asked.

"Right under us. We're standing on it." Seth looked

down. He was standing on a clam shell. It was huge, though Seth knew that when he was his normal human size he could have held the clam in his hand.

"A clam!" he exclaimed. "Just like the ones at the beach."

"Yep, but the more proper term is 'mussel,'" Mattie explained.

"Do these have pearls in them?"

"Some mussels will produce pearls, but only if something small, like a grain of sand, gets lodged in it. Then the pearl is formed around the sand."

"Hey, let's look inside him! I've never looked inside a live clam—uh, mussel—before. Maybe I can find a pearl!"

"I don't know if we can open it because they keep the two valves of their shells tightly shut. But you can try to pry them apart."

Seth knelt down and stuck his hands in the small gap between the two halves of the mussel's shell.

"Ummmmph!" he uttered as he struggled to pull the valves apart. He pulled with all his might, but the two halves would not budge. Seth was disappointed.

"You'll just have to wait until you're back to your normal size. Then you'll have the strength to open one," Mattie said.

"Yeah, I guess you're right." They were about to leave when Seth saw the valves begin to move apart. "Hey Mattie! They're moving!" Seth crawled back down to the mussel and peeked inside. Slowly the mussel opened wide enough that Seth could crawl inside for a better look.

"Seth, I wouldn't do that if I were you. If it decides to close its valves, you could get trapped inside."

"Oh, please," Seth smirked. "I'm quicker than this old slow-poke. I can get out if he starts to close up."

"Okay, but don't say I didn't warn you," Mattie said. The inside of the mussel was a light pink color and very squishy. "The inside of the mussel is called the mantle," Mattie said. Seth held up a flap with several slits in it.

"What's this?" he asked Mattie.

"Those are his gills. In addition to using them for breathing, they also use the gills to filter food particles out of the water."

"It's gooey," Seth said as he wrinkled his nose.

"That's because they are covered in a mucous* that traps the food." Seth crawled further back into the mussel, and was now completely inside of it. He was so busy probing around that he didn't notice when it began to close its shell. "Seth! He's closing up! Get out of there!" Mattie yelled. Seth turned around to crawl out, but his foot got stuck in between the mantle and the shell.

"Mattie!" Seth screamed. "My foot's stuck! Help me!" Mattie reached in to grab Seth's foot, but it was too late. The mussel closed its valves, with Seth trapped inside. Seth began banging on the shell. "HELP! Mattie, get me out of here!" he cried.

"I can't do anything," Mattie said desperately. "I'm not strong enough to pry it open!"

Seth's heart began to race and he started to sweat. *Don't panic*, he told himself. *Don't panic*. Seth's dad had

Pronounced: "MYOO-kus"

always taught him to keep his cool in a sticky situation, and Seth was literally in a sticky situation. If you didn't panic, Seth's dad always said, a solution to the problem would usually come to you. *Remain calm. You can get yourself out of here.* He thought for a minute.

"Seth! Seth!" Mattie cried. "What are you doing?"

"I'm trying not to panic, Mattie," Seth replied as calmly as he could. But he wasn't feeling very calm. In fact, his hands were shaking a little bit. Seth was scared, but he was not about to give up. "And I'm thinking. I'm trying to figure out how to get out of here."

The little mayfly began to panic. "Ohhhh, your mom is going to kill me," he whined. He looked around. "Maybe I can find a stick to pry open the valves."

"That's a good idea, Mattie," Seth said. He could tell the mayfly was freaking out, so looking for a stick would keep him occupied while Seth figured out a solution to his problem.

Suddenly an idea came to Seth. He remembered when he had tickled Penny's gills, and he wondered if mussels were ticklish, too. *It's worth a shot*, he thought. He began tickling the area beneath him, but nothing happened. He moved over a little bit and tried again. Still nothing.

Seth's heart raced a little faster. *"Stay calm under pressure, son,"* Seth could hear his dad saying.

"Seth! Seth, can you hear me?" Mattie asked. "I can't find any sticks small enough for me to pick up. And even if I could, they would be too small to pry open the mussel. I don't know what to do!" Mattie was sounding desperate.

"Yes, Mattie, I can hear you. I had an idea. I'm trying to tickle the mussel. Maybe that will make it open up," he replied. "But it's not working yet." It was beginning to get very hot inside the shell. Seth was also a bit claustrophobic; he hated small places.

"Seth! That's brilliant!" Mattie exclaimed. "I have heard that mussels are very ticklish, especially at the back, where the two valves are hinged. Why didn't I think of that?" The little mayfly slapped his forehead in his ignorance.

Seth moved to the very back of the shell, near the hinge, and tickled right along the base of the shell. The mantle began rolling beneath him. Seth saw the valves open just a bit. He tickled the area more furiously. The valves opened a little more and before he knew what happened, Seth was spit out of the mussel, covered in mucous.

"Seth! You're alive!" Mattie ran over and gave him a hug, then immediately released Seth, shaking his leg in the water. "Whoa, you got slimed!" Mattie exclaimed.

Seth wiped the back of his hand over his head and shook off a large ball of mucous. "Thanks for pointing that out, Mattie. I hadn't noticed," Seth answered sarcastically.

"You know, you're very lucky to have gotten out of there with only a little slime on you."

"I know," Seth sighed. "I know." His legs were still trembling.

"Are you okay?" Mattie asked. "That was a pretty scary experience."

Seth took a deep breath. "Yeah, I'm okay. Just a little shaken up, that's all. But everything's okay, I'm fine," he said. "I didn't find a pearl, though."

"If you'd gotten stuck in there, you might've become a pearl," Mattie said. "Let's move along downstream."

"Yeah, I think that's a good idea," Seth said, "I don't care if I ever see another mussel for the rest of my life."

-10-

The Old Tree Trunk

Mattie and Seth continued crawling along the rocks, when it suddenly became very dark. Seth looked up to see a large gelatinous mass floating near the surface of the water. It was growing on several large stems that were sticking out of an old tree trunk. Seth recognized the mass to be the bryozoans he'd seen yesterday with his dad.

"Hey, Mattie," he said, "those are bryozoans growing above us, aren't they?"

"Yes they are. How'd you know that? Wait. Let me guess, your dad taught you," Mattie said.

"Yep," Seth said. "I caught one yesterday while we were fishing."

"How does your dad know about all this stuff?" Mattie asked.

"He's a biologist. He counts fish in the rivers, but he also knows a lot about the invertebrates, too. Can we go look at the bryozoans up close? He told me that we can't see them without a microscope, but I bet I can see them now since I'm so small."

"You're right, you can see them now, but it's kinda dangerous to get up there. We'd have to climb on the stems—that's dragonfly territory," Mattie replied.

"Oh yeah, we did see a dragonfly on the stem yesterday with the bryozoans," Seth answered. A disappointed look crossed his face. Mattie could see that Seth really wanted to get a better look at the bryozoans.

"Okay," he said, "we can go up there, but we've got to be very, *very* careful. The first sign of a dragonfly, and we come back down, okay?"

"Really?! You mean we can go up there? Oh, Mattie, you're the best!" Seth exclaimed. They swam over to the bank of the river, where the large tree trunk sat.

"Now we're going to be getting into some stronger current up here, so you need to be extra careful and make sure you have a good grip on the stem," Mattie warned.

"Okay," Seth said. Mattie climbed up on the trunk with Seth right behind him. Very carefully they made their way up, up, up. Seth felt the current ripping at his clothes. "Mattie, I feel like I'm slipping," he said. Mattie looked back at Seth. He had both arms wrapped completely around the twig he was on. Mattie was concerned and began looking for a place that was more protected.

"If you can hang on for just a bit longer, there is a place up here that we can get out of the current. Do you think you can do that?"

"I think so," Seth replied.

"Please be careful," Mattie begged. Mattie watched as Seth cautiously made his way to Mattie. Mattie breathed a sigh of relief. This was much more difficult than he had thought it would be. "Okay, that's where we're going." He pointed to a small blob of bryozoans that were hidden in a small cove in the bank.

"Wow, we're up high," Seth said. He looked up. "We're almost out of the water!"

"Just wait," Matte said, "we're going even higher. The view from the top should be fantastic. You're not afraid of heights, are you?" Mattie asked.

"No, but I was just about to ask you the same question," Seth answered.

"I don't know if I'm afraid of heights," Mattie replied. "I've never been this high up before." They continued their climb, protected from the current by a large branch. It wasn't long before they reached the top of the tree trunk, where Mattie had earlier spotted the smaller clump of bryozoans. The surface of the water wasn't far above their heads now.

"This is it," Mattie said. They turned around and gazed upon the river below them. To his right he could see the riffle from which he and Mattie had just come. He could just barely see the lush patch of moss where Old Griswald lived, and if he looked closely, he could even make out Harry's home. To his left was the large, deep pool where he often swam. The water was so clear that he could see all the way to the bottom. Halfway across the pool the water turned a deep turquoise, at which point Seth could see no further. All was quiet except for a small school of minnows searching for food near the opposite bank. "It's beautiful, isn't it?" Mattie asked. For the first time in his life, Seth was nearly speechless. Words could not describe how beautiful the river looked.

"Wow," Seth said, "this view is awesome." Seth looked up at the bryozoan colony and saw something U-shaped waving in the current. "There's the crown of tentacles!" he exclaimed. But he spotted something even more interesting out of the corner of his eye. It was *inside* the mass of bryozoans. Seth pressed his face against the gelatinous blob to get a better look. "Look! There's a worm eating the bryozoans! And it's green!" The worm was turned away from Seth, munching on some algae that was growing along with the bryozoan, unaware it was being watched.

Mattie took a closer look. "That's not a worm, that's a fly larva. It's a kind of fly called a midge," he said.

"A fly larva! Mattie, flies are insects! This can't be an insect, it doesn't have six legs."

"This is a good example of the variation that can be seen within the insects. Some insects don't have any legs as larvae. Some, like this midge, have prolegs,* which aren't true legs, but are just fleshy stubs with claws at the end for holding onto things. You can see he has two prolegs—they're right below his head. He also has two prolegs at the far end of his body. Those are used for holding onto things, too. He uses the prolegs for crawling around, sort of like an inchworm."

"I still don't see how you can call that thing an insect," Seth said.

"If you could see an adult, you would believe me because it has six legs and wings," Mattie said.

"How does it *sprout* legs?" Seth asked in disbelief.

"It will become a pupa and metamorphose into an adult midge, complete with legs and wings, just like Penny. Remember?"

*Pronounced: *"PROH-legs"*

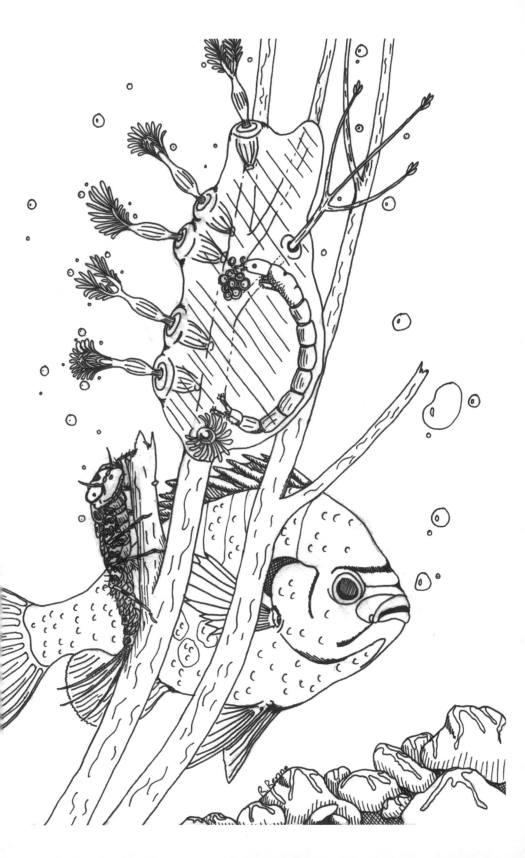

Seth thought back to their conversation with Penny. "But Penny already had legs," he insisted. "How is Penny like this midge?"

"It's still a similar process—lots of cool things happen during metamorphosis that even I don't understand," Mattie said. "Basically their entire body gets torn down and re-built into a completely different looking insect, like a caterpillar turning into a butterfly."

"What about you, Mattie? Do you undergo metamorphosis?"

"Nope," Mattie replied matter-of-factly. "I simply keep growing bigger and bigger until it's time for me to leave the water as an adult. Then I crawl out of the water, and my wings—" Mattie looked over his shoulder—"my wings will sprout from these wingpads on my back."

"Huh," Seth said skeptically. "That's weird. I mean, metamorphosis sounds kinda cool, but *this* thing isn't very exciting, at least not right now," Seth said.

"Well, they probably aren't the most exciting creatures living in the river, but they are one of the most abundant," Mattie answered. "If you get down deep enough in the sediments, you can find hundreds of them."

"Why is it green?" Seth asked.

"Their body color is usually determined by what they eat. They eat a lot of algae so that's why they look green," Mattie explained.

"I'm glad my skin color isn't determined by what I eat because I'd look like a rainbow!" he said, thinking about the different foods he ate like carrots, macaroni and cheese, spinach, and blueberries.

Mattie laughed. "That would look kinda funny. I think we'd better be moving along now. I'm starting to get a little nervous about being so high up."

"Okay, but one last look at the river while we're here," Seth suggested. He took one long, last look at the river. He'd been swimming in this river a hundred times before, but there was just something different, even mystical, from a mayfly's perspective. It was a totally different world, a world he didn't even know existed before today.

"Are you ready now?" Mattie asked. He was beginning to get more nervous. "I'm ready to get my claws back on solid rock. And I'm a little concerned that we haven't seen at least one dragonfly yet. That makes me wonder if they're up to something."

"Maybe they're out hunting somewhere else in the river," Seth said.

"It's possible," Mattie said, "but not likely. C'mon, let's get outta here." They began their descent. About halfway down the tree trunk a large shadow passed over them. Seth and Mattie both dodged into a clump of moss. It was a longear sunfish. "Oh yeah," Mattie said, "we also have to look out for fish predators."

"I'd forgotten about the fish," Seth said. "I guess you don't have to worry much about that when you're under the rocks, huh?"

"For the most part, no, but there are some small fish that can get between the cracks in the rocks and those we do have to worry about," Mattie explained.

"Boy, I guess no place is truly safe around here," Seth said.

"They are few and far between. Like Harry said, never a dull moment," Mattie confirmed. They waited for the sunfish to pass, then resumed their descent. They were nearly down when Seth's foot slipped. "OH, NO!" Seth yelled. "HELP!" He lunged for the stem, but it was useless. The current ripped him away and he went tumbling downstream. Mattie watched helplessly as Seth disappeared down the river.

-11-

Callie

Seth tumbled head over heels for several seconds before he was able to upright himself. He had never been so terrified in his entire life. He wondered if he would ever see his parents again. Or Llama! He couldn't bear to think such bad thoughts. He felt tears begin to well up in his eyes. *Stop it, Seth*, he told himself. *You have to stay calm and figure out how to get yourself out of this mess.* As he watched the river blur past, he knew his only hope was to make it to the next pool where the current would be slower. There he could swim down to the riverbed and, hopefully, crawl back upstream to Mattie. It was a long shot, he knew, but it was the only chance he had. The tricky part would be getting through the pool without being eaten by a fish.

Seth spotted something ahead in his path that he didn't want to see—a large rock covered with plants. He was headed straight for it, and it was too late to maneuver out of the way. *Smack!* Seth was broad-sided by a huge leaf. He winced. *That stung*, he thought. The blow knocked Seth into a wild spin, sending him into a side channel where the current wasn't so swift. He relaxed a little bit. Now he had time to think about a plan that would get him out of the current. As he swam toward the bank, he got caught in a swirling eddy, which sucked him down and spun him around several times.

Before he could work his way out of the spin, he suddenly got caught in something. It took him a second to realize that he had stopped moving. When he looked around to see what he'd gotten caught in, he saw that it was some sort of net, sort of like a spider web. It was wide and funnel-shaped and led to a dark hole. Seth didn't know what kind of net it was, or who it belonged to, but thoughts of mean, hungry predators flashed through his mind. He quickly made his way toward the opening, not wanting to find out who it belonged to.

"Who's there?" a voice asked. Seth froze in his tracks. Should he answer or keep going? "Oh, my gosh! You're human!" the voice said.

Seth decided the voice did not sound like that of a vicious predator. He turned around to see a strange-looking creature peeking out of the dark hole at the back of the net.

"How did you get in the river? And how—how did you get to be so small?" The creature crawled out of its hole for a better look at Seth.

"I met Mattie the mayfly this morning and he took me on a tour of the river—at least until we got separated," Seth said.

"You mean you're alone?" the creature asked. "How long have you been separated from your friend?"

"Long enough," Seth replied. "I slipped while we were climbing down the big tree trunk, and got swept downstream. Then I got caught in your web."

"Oh, you poor thing, you must be scared to death."

Seth summoned all the courage he had in his body, all the way up from his toes, and held his head high. "I'm not scared," he said defensively. But he could tell the creature didn't believe him. He shrugged his shoulders. "Well, maybe just a little scared."

"Well, don't worry. I'll help you find your way back to Mattie, okay? By the way, my name's Callie. What's your name?"

"My name is Seth. I'm glad I ran into you because I'm ready to go home."

Seth took a closer look at Callie. He'd never seen anything like her before. She had six legs, so he knew she was an insect. But she had a long, cylindrical body that was covered in what he thought were gills, and she lived inside a house made of twigs with a large net as a front porch. "Callie, can I ask you a question?" he asked.

"Of course," Callie answered. "Ask me anything you want."

"Well, I've been learning about all the different invertebrates that live in the river, and I know you're an insect because you have six legs. But I have no idea what kind of insect you are."

Callie smiled warmly. "I'm a caddisfly," she replied. She like Seth's curiosity.

"You look kinda like the fly larva I just saw—I think it was a midge?" Seth said, unsure if he remembered correctly. "Only you have all of your legs."

"I guess I sort of look like a midge," Callie said thoughtfully. "But there's lots of ways to tell caddisflies apart from midges. The first, of course, is that we have all of our legs. Many midges have only prolegs or no legs at all. Another way to tell us apart is by looking at our thorax,"* Callie said.

"What's a *thorax*?" Seth asked.

"Mattie didn't teach you about the body parts of an insect?" Callie asked.

"No," Seth said, shaking his head.

"Well then, I guess it's time you learned. An insect has

*Pronounced: *"THOR-aks"*

three regions of its body." She pointed to each region on her body. "A head," she smiled. "That one's obvious—a thorax and an abdomen.* The thorax is made up of the first three segments behind the head. It's similar to your chest. This is where our legs are—we have one pair of legs on each segment." She waved her legs around in the water. "The abdomen is all the rest of the segments of the body. It's like your stomach."

Seth nodded. "Okay, I get it. So what's so special about your thorax?" he asked.

"Well, most caddisflies have hardened plates on their thorax. The first segment is always covered with a large plate, but then the second and third segments can vary from having large plates to having no plates at all. True flies, such as the midge you just saw, don't have large hardened plates on their thorax. In fact, lots of times all three of their thoracic** segments are fused together into one large segment, like a giant turtleneck sweater."

Seth peered at Callie's thorax. "All of yours are covered with large plates."

"That's right. Our abdomen is never covered with hardened plates, but sometimes it's covered with gills, like mine," Callie said.

---

*Pronounced: *"AB-doh-men"*
**Pronounced: *"THOR-a-sick"*

"I had guessed those were gills!" Seth said excitedly.

"You won't find a midge with gills all over its abdomen," Callie said. "Besides, how many midges do you know who build cases and nets?"

"Huh?" Seth asked.

"That's what we caddisflies do," Callie answered. "Some of us build cases to live in, and others of us build nets, like the one you got caught in, to capture food."

"Oh, you mean your web? I thought it was your front porch." Seth paused in thought. "Wait. Did you say you catch food in this thing?"

"I sure do. In fact, I thought you might have been my lunch, but you shook my entire net when you landed so I knew you were too big for me to eat. I thought you might have been a fish."

"So you have a net, but not a case? What's a case?" Seth asked. He was confused.

"A case is basically a caddisfly's house. I don't have a case. I only have a net. But you can see some caddisflies dragging around large cases made of sand, rocks, or sticks. My neighbor has a case. Here, I'll show you what they look like."

Callie and Seth went outside and Callie called to her

neighbor. "Oh, Brad!" Seth watched as a bunch of rocks moved and to his surprise, a caddisfly popped his head out of the rocks.

"It's like a sleeping bag!" Seth exclaimed.

"Yeah," Callie said. "I guess it is. Brad, I'd like you to meet my new human friend, Seth. He would like to see your case."

"Hello, Seth," Brad said. "Pleasure to meet you."

"Hello," said Seth. "You have a very pretty case. Is it heavy?"

"Not in the water," Brad answered. "I can go just about anywhere. But oh boy, I would hate to have to drag it across dry ground! The real trick is not to get stuck between the rocks."

"That must be scary. I'd hate to have to worry about getting stuck between the rocks all the time." Seth paused. "I have a question. Your case is just big enough for you to fit in now. And surely you can't drag that thing around when you're a baby caddisfly. So what happens to your case when you molt?" Seth asked.

Brad looked surprised. "He's a smart kid, huh, Callie?"

"Yes, he is," Callie replied.

"I've been learning about insects all day," Seth said proudly.

"Well, to answer your question, when I molt I throw away my old case and build a new, bigger one to live in."

"Wow, that's a lot of work," Seth said. "But really cool! So only caddisflies build cases?"

"That's right," Callie said proudly. "We are unique among the insects."

"And what about your net? Do all caddisflies build nets?" Seth asked.

"No, some caddisflies actively hunt for their food," Callie answered. "So they don't build cases or nets."

"You mean they're predators," Seth said nervously. "So what kind of stuff do you catch in your net?"

"Oh, I catch mostly algae, but sometimes I get some really small animals," Callie said. "Those are special treats." Suddenly Callie saw a large shadow move behind a rock. "Quick, let's move back into my net," she said, moving toward the back of her net.

"What's wrong?" Seth asked.

"Something moved out there and I don't know what it was. I just want to be careful and keep you out of sight of any dragonflies or fish," she said.

"Good-bye, Brad," Seth said quickly. "It was nice to meet you and learn about your case."

"Good-bye. Be careful out there," Brad replied as he drew himself deep within his case.

Callie pulled Seth close to her thorax, wrapped her legs tightly around his body, and waited.

-12-

Pauli

The shadow grew larger and then stopped just out-side Callie's net. Seth held his breath. *Please don't be a dragonfly*, he thought to himself. *Please, anything but a dragonfly.* The creature moved in front of the net where Seth could see it. "MATTIE!" he yelled, scrambling to get out of Callie's legs.

"Seth! No!" Callie cautioned. But Seth was already out of her legs and making his way toward the front of the net.

"Mattie! It's me, Seth!" he yelled. The creature turned and faced Seth—only it wasn't Mattie. Seth couldn't hide his disappointment. "You're not Mattie!" He burst into tears.

"Whoa, whoa," the newcomer said. "I've never had anybody cry when they met me. What's the problem?"

Callie crawled out to where Seth was standing and comforted him. She turned to the newcomer. "Hi, I'm Callie. This is Seth. He's been separated from his friend Mattie the mayfly."

"Oh, I see," the creature said. "My name's Pauli. I'm a stonefly."

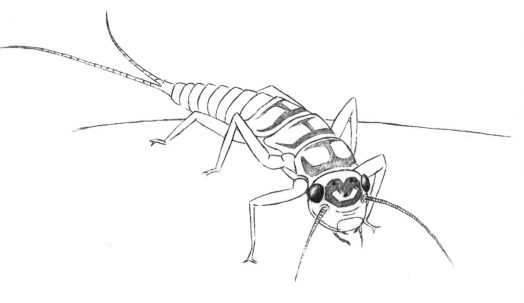

"It's nice to meet you, Pauli," Callie said.

Seth looked up and wiped the tears from his eyes. "You look just like Mattie," he said. "I thought I was going home."

"I'm sorry to disappoint you, Seth. People confuse me with mayflies all the time. I guess I'm going to have to start wearing a name tag," Pauli said.

"So how do I tell you apart from Mattie?" Seth asked, his voice cracking. "Oh wait," Seth looked closely at Pauli. " You only have two tails—Mattie has three. And your gills are different than his."

"You're right, I do only have two tails, but you have to be careful because some mayflies also have only two tails. And my gills are different because they aren't on my abdomen. I have tufts of gills on my thorax, almost in my armpits. But the way you can definitely tell the difference between stoneflies and mayflies is by looking at our claws. I have two claws on each leg, but Mattie only has one claw on each leg. To someone who's never seen a stonefly before, I can understand how you got confused," Pauli said.

"You do look an awful lot alike," Seth sniffled.

"If you don't mind me asking, how did you get separated from Mattie?"

"Well, we had climbed up the big tree trunk to look at the bryozoans and we were on our way down when my foot slipped and I got swept downstream," Seth answered.

"Oh, so you're from upstream, are ya?" Pauli asked. "Well, it just so happens that I'm on my way to visit my brother who lives upstream past the old tree trunk. If you like, you can join me and I'll help you find Mattie."

Seth gasped. "Really!? You'll help me find Mattie?" He gave Pauli a huge hug. "Oh, thank you, thank you, THANK YOU!"

"Easy now, we haven't found Mattie yet," Pauli said.

Seth turned back to Callie. "Callie, thank you for not

being a big mean predator and eating me when I crashed into your net."

Callie laughed so hard her gills trembled. "Ah, Seth," she sighed. "You are so cute. I'm glad you came crashing into my net. It was really nice to meet you. Come here." She held her arms open for a hug. As she and Seth embraced, she tickled him with her gills.

Seth shrieked and squirmed to get away, but with six legs wrapped around his body, he was going nowhere fast. "Callie! Stop it! Please!"

Callie gave Seth a final tickle, then released him. "I suppose I've teased you enough," she said. Callie turned to Pauli. "Pauli, please take good care of him, okay?"

"Yes, ma'am," he replied.

"Good luck in finding Mattie. And watch out for dragonflies," she warned.

"We'd better be moving along, Seth," Pauli said. "It's getting late and we have a long road ahead of us."

"Okay," Seth said. "Bye, Callie. Thanks again for everything." Then he and Pauli began their difficult and dangerous trek upstream.

-13-

The Dragonfly

"So where does your brother live?" Seth asked as they climbed down into a small crevice between two rocks.

"If you go on past the old tree trunk, then it's about another half day's journey from there. It's near a huge rock in the middle of the river," Pauli replied.

"The huge rock! That's my rock!" Seth exclaimed. "That's the one I lie on all the time! I know exactly where that is. It's the best rock in the whole river!" He missed that rock. He longed for the days of lying on it and looking for cloud cartoons.

Seth and Pauli had been walking for what seemed like forever. "Can we take a break?" Seth asked. "I'm tired of walking."

"Sure," Pauli said. "We've made good time, so we can stop for a few minutes." They sat down on a rock that was slightly sheltered from the current.

"Have you ever seen a dragonfly before?" Seth asked.

"Oh sure, I've seen my share of dragonflies," Pauli said. "I've never had a close encounter with one myself,

96

but I've seen other insects get eaten by dragonflies. It's not a pretty sight."

Seth shuddered. "I hope I don't see one while I'm still in the river," he said.

"How are you doing?" Pauli asked once they had been resting for a while. "Are you ready to walk again?"

Seth stood up. "Yes, I'm ready. Let's go. I'm ready to find Mattie."

They continued their trek, climbing over rocks and between large cracks in the rocks, trying the whole time to stay as low as possible. That way they were better protected from predators and the current was weaker. The last thing Seth wanted was to get caught in the current again. He'd had enough of that kind of excitement to last him the rest of his life. Although they had been crawling down between the rocks, Seth had not seen many other invertebrates in a very long time. He thought this was kind of strange.

"Pauli, why haven't we seen many other animals lately?" he asked nervously.

"I was just wondering that myself," Pauli replied. "It's very unusual. This place is usually teeming with life. I don't get it."

"It's kinda creepy, if you ask me," Seth said.

"It is a bit unsettling," Pauli agreed. "But I don't think it's anything we need to worry about." Then the water became very still. All was quiet.

"I don't like this, Pauli," Seth said.

"I don't like it, either," Pauli replied. "Let's try to get out of here as quickly as possible." Seth followed Pauli as quickly as he could, but as he was making his way through one tiny opening, his foot got stuck between two rocks.

"Pauli! Wait up! My foot is stuck." He reached back to pull it out. It was wedged in tightly. Pauli came back to help. Pauli tugged on Seth's leg, but with no success.

"Let me find a stick and we'll pry it out," he suggested. "I'll be right back." He swam away to find a stick.

Seth leaned up against a rock to rest. *This is just what we need*, he thought, *something to slow us down.* He sighed and thought back to Brad the caddisfly and his large case. *Well, at lest I'm not dragging a bunch of rocks around*, he thought. He felt a swirl of water behind him. "Pauli? Is that you?" He turned around, expecting to see Pauli prying his foot out with a stick. What he saw instead nearly scared him to death—a dragonfly! And it was right in his face! "Aggghhhhh!" he screamed. He yanked hard

on his foot, but it would not give. He wiggled his foot, trying to loosen it from the rock, hoping it would pop out.
Seth saw the large, lower lip of the dragonfly lurch toward
his head. He gave one final hard tug on his foot, and it gave
way, scraping along the rock as it came out. He fell for-
ward, the dragonfly's lip just missing the back of his head.
He scrambled to a small opening under a rock, hoping it
was too small for the dragonfly to follow. Seth was trembling. *Where is Pauli?* he wondered. He hoped Pauli was
in a safe place. Seth could see the dragonfly's shadow outside the opening. *Good*, he thought, *he can't get in here.*

Then Seth saw two legs inching toward him, sweep-
ing the ground, searching for prey. Seth pressed himself against the back wall of his refuge, hoping it was far
enough back so that the dragonfly's legs couldn't reach
him. He had no other way out, so he was forced to wait
until the dragonfly gave up. Or at least Seth hoped it
would give up. He curled up into the tiniest ball possible,
with his legs pulled against his chest, and rested his chin
on his knees. It was only then that Seth felt the searing
pain in his foot from when he scraped it across the rock.
He winced. How much skin had he left behind on the
rock? It must have been a lot, given the amount of pain.

The dragonfly waited outside the opening for a very long time. *Why won't that thing just give up?* he wondered. He grew weary of watching the shadow and shut his eyes. He realized how tired he felt. Eventually Seth dozed off.

When he awoke, he no longer saw the hulking shadow. He didn't know how long he'd been asleep. Had the dragonfly finally given up? Seth decided to wait a while longer to make sure that the dragonfly had given up for good. Several minutes later he saw another shadow outside the opening.

"Seth? Are you in here?" a voice asked. It was Pauli!

"Yes! I'm here!" Seth replied.

"It's safe to come out now. The dragonfly's given up on you."

Seth crawled out of his hiding place. "Are you sure he's gone?"

"I'm positive. I watched him leave."

"How did you know I was in there?" Seth asked.

"When I came back with the stick to pry out your foot, I saw him nearly rip your head off. As soon as I saw that you were safe, I hid in a place where I could watch him," Pauli replied. "He was very persistent. He must have wanted to eat you badly, because he waited longer than I've ever seen any dragonfly stalk its prey."

"I thought I was that guy's lunch," Seth said. "I don't think I've ever been that scared in my life. That even beats getting swept downstream."

"Well, I can't guarantee that he won't come back looking for you, so we'd better get out of here fast," Pauli suggested.

"Not a problem," Seth said as he turned and climbed onto a rock.

They resumed their journey upstream. Seth was beginning to tire, his feet dragging more and more. Pauli noticed the trip was wearing on Seth. "Would you like to take another break?" he asked.

"No, I'm okay. Just a little tired, that's all. I'll be okay. If we don't stop, we'll get there that much quicker."

"Okay," Pauli said. "Let me know if you need to rest, though." Seth's eyes were glazed over. He wasn't even listening anymore. He put himself on auto-pilot and just trudged along after Pauli.

After plodding along for awhile in silence, Seth looked up and let out a loud yell. "Yahoo!" he yelled, jumping up and down, pointing to something in the distance. "Would you look at that!" Pauli followed Seth's finger to a large, dark figure in the distance. "It's the old tree trunk!" Seth yelled. "We're almost there!" He had a surge in energy and took off swimming as fast as he could.

"Seth! Be careful. We are still a long way from the tree trunk. You don't want to wear yourself out," Pauli cautioned.

"I've got plenty of energy now!" he yelled back to Pauli, who was struggling to keep up with Seth. Seth stopped and waited for Pauli. "C'mon, where's your energy?" he teased.

"Patience, my boy," Pauli said. "We'll get there in good time."

"That's what my dad always says. That, and 'a watched pot never boils,'" he said in his best father-like voice.

Pauli smiled. "He's right, you know." Seth rolled his eyes. "Don't worry, Seth. It won't be too much longer." Seth knew this—that's why he was leading the way.

Return to Harry's

It was not long before the old tree trunk was looming over them and Seth began to recognize where he was. "Pauli, this is it! We're almost there!" He suddenly realized he didn't have a clue as to how he would find Mattie. He didn't even know where Mattie lived. "Oh no," he said.

"What's the matter?" Pauli asked. "This is where we're supposed to be, right?"

"Yeah, but I don't know how to find Mattie. I don't even know where he lives."

"Well, do you know anyone who would know where he lives?" Pauli asked.

"Harry!" Seth exclaimed. "I know where his cousin Harry lives!"

"What are we waiting for, then?" Pauli asked. "Let's find Harry!" Seth led the way to Harry's house, hardly able to contain his excitement.

"Harry! Harry!" Seth called once he reached Harry's home. "It's Seth!"

Harry came outside with a confused look on his

face. "What are you doing here?" he asked. "Where's Mattie?"

"We got separated. I fell off the old tree trunk and got swept downstream. But I came back so Mattie could send me home."

"Yes, I know. Mattie told me what happened. That's why he went to look for you."

"What?" Seth asked in disbelief.

"Mattie went to look for you downstream. He formed a search party right after you got swept away."

"Oh, no!" Seth moaned. "No, no, no! I can't believe we missed him! Now I may never get to go home!" He fought back tears.

"Now don't worry, Seth," Pauli said. "We'll find Mattie. Don't you worry."

Harry thought quickly. "Okay, Seth, I've got a plan. I have another mayfly friend who's one of the strongest swimmers in the river. I'll have him track down Mattie. Why don't you and your friend rest in my house and I'll take care of everything."

"I really must be going," Pauli said. "I still have a long road ahead of me. I just wanted to make sure Seth made it back safely. It looks like matters are beyond my control now."

"Thank you for letting me come with you, Pauli," Seth said. "You're the coolest stonefly I've ever met."

"And the only stonefly you've ever met, too," Pauli said.

Seth smiled. "Well, that, too," he said. "Good-bye, Pauli."

"Good-bye, Seth," Pauli said as he swam away. "Good luck!"

Harry returned quickly. "Seth, I've sent my friend off to find Mattie for us. Don't worry. He'll find him soon." Seth nodded his head. His eyes were drooping—he was tired from his trip. "Why don't you come in my house and rest while we wait for Mattie?" Harry said.

"Okay," he said. He followed Harry inside and snuggled up in a corner on a bed of moss. Soon Seth drifted off to sleep with visions of home in his head.

-15-

Seth Goes Home

Seth awoke to the sound of voices. For a second he forgot where he was. Then he remembered that he was still in the river, waiting for Mattie to return. He crawled out of the bed of moss and peeked into the other room from which the voices were coming. "MATTIE!" Seth yelled. "You're back!" He ran over to the mayfly and attacked him with a bear hug. "I thought I'd never see you again! How long have I been asleep? And why didn't you wake me up?"

"I just got here. You thought you'd never see *me* again? I thought I'd never see *you* again, crazy kid. Why did you have to go slipping off that stem for, anyway? You nearly gave me a heart attack."

Seth shrugged his shoulders. "I guess things just weren't exciting enough. But I took care of that, didn't I?" Seth said with a mischievous grin. "Like Harry always says, 'Never a dull moment in this river.'"

"I didn't mean you had to create your own excitement, Seth," Harry said.

"So what did you see downstream?" Mattie asked. "How did you get back?"

"Well, I crashed into a caddisfly's net after I got smacked upside the head by a leaf, then I met a stone-fly—he brought me back up here, then I was nearly eaten by a dragonfly. . . ."

"WHAT?" Mattie gasped. "You were nearly eaten by a dragonfly?"

"Yep," Seth answered. "That's why I have these scrapes on my foot." He pointed down to his right foot, which had bright pink streaks running along the top and outside edge.

"Ouch!" Mattie said. "That looks like it hurts."

"It stings a little bit," Seth said. "But it's not like I lost my entire leg."

Mattie smiled. "Good point. But I think you need to take care of those scrapes. It's time for you to go home, huh?" Mattie said.

Seth nodded. "I'm ready to go home," he said. "But I've had such a great day! I learned so much about invertebrates and insects. I can't wait to tell my dad about all the cool things I saw today!"

"I'm glad you've enjoyed your trip down the river, Seth. I've enjoyed showing you around. Maybe you can teach your friends about all of us down here."

"Oh, for sure!" Seth said. "My friends will think you guys are so cool!" Seth looked Mattie in the eye. "I'll miss you, Mattie."

"I'll miss you, too, Seth," Mattie replied. "Remember, you're welcome down here anytime."

Seth grinned. "Thanks. I'll come back and visit, I promise." Seth turned to Harry. "Bye, Harry . . . again. Thanks for sending your friend to find Mattie."

"It was no problem. I'm just glad you got back here safely," Harry replied.

"Well, Seth. I guess this is good-bye," Mattie said.

"Yeah, I guess so. Tell me what I have to do so I can go home."

"All you have to do is spin around three times and say, 'Mattie is the greatest mayfly ever,'" Mattie teased.

"What?" Seth asked. "You're kidding, right?"

"Yeah, I am. Seriously, all you gotta do is close your eyes and count to five."

"Okay." Seth closed his eyes. "Five . . . four . . . three . . . two . . . ONE." When he opened his eyes he was still staring Mattie in the face. Seth panicked. "What happened? It didn't work!"

"Duh, it didn't work. I said count *to* five, not count

backwards from five. It's just the opposite of what you did this morning."

"Oh," Seth said sheepishly. "Let's try this again." He closed his eyes. "One . . . two . . . three . . . four . . . FIVE." Seth felt the same strange sensation come over his body as he did earlier that morning. *It's working!* he thought.

When Seth opened his eyes, he was lying on his rock. Dazed, he propped himself up on his elbows and tried to remember what he had been dreaming about. Talking mayflies. Shrinking to the size of a bug. Breathing underwater. Being chased by a hungry dragonfly! Seth laughed. *What a weird dream*, he thought to himself. Dad will get a kick out of that one! Seth crawled off the rock and stepped in the water. He cringed and sucked in a breath of air. "Owwwww! That stings!" he yelped. He looked down to see several scrapes along the top of his foot. *Wow, that must have been some wild dream I had*, Seth thought.

Or was it really a dream?

Cast of Characters

The Bryozoan ....

Mattie ......

Penny ....

Norris ....

Harry ....

Old Griswald ....

The Mussel ....

The Midge ....

Callie ....

Pauli ....

The Dragonfly ....

The Bryozoan:

PHYLUM[1] BRYOZOA[2]

(THE MOSS ANIMALS)

Ecology: Bryozoans are filter-feeding colonial animals with a U-shaped ring of tentacles around the mouth that draws water toward them from which they filter small food particles. The finely branched look of the tentacles give them the common name 'moss animals.' They secrete a gooey, gelatinous substance around themselves that helps join neighbors together in the colony.

Cool fact: Since Bryozoans can't move, they defend themselves in various ways, such as growing spines or producing poisons that are toxic to fish.

[1] Pronounced: *"FYE-lum"*   [2] Pronounced: *"bry-uh-ZOE-uh"*

Mattie:

PHYLUM ARTHROPODA[1]
CLASS INSECTA[2]
ORDER EPHEMEROPTERA[3]
FAMILY HEPTAGENIIDAE[4]
GENUS *STENONEMA*[5] (CREAM CAHILL)

Ecology: Mayflies are found in freshwater streams, rivers, lakes, and marshes with plenty of dissolved oxygen. Mayflies that live in running waters are flattened so they will resist the pull of water currents as they crawl around on the rocks. Most mayflies are scrapers, eating algae, diatoms,[6] and other plants off of rocks, but some can filter small food particles from the water with specialized bristles on their front set of legs.

Cool fact: Mayfly nymphs can live for two years in a river, but the adults live only for a few days at most. In fact, adults don't even have mouthparts!

[1] Pronounced: *"ARE-throw-PODE-uh"*
[2] Pronounced: *"in-SEK-tuh"*
[3] Pronounced: *"ee-FEM-er-OPP-ter-uh"*
[4] Pronounced: *"HEP-tih-jen-NAE-ih-dee"*
[5] Pronounced: *"sten-oh-NEE-muh"* [3]
[6] Pronounced: *"DYE-uh-toms"*

Penny:

PHYLUM ARTHROPODA
CLASS INSECTA
ORDER COLEOPTERA[1]
FAMILY PSEPHENIDAE[2]
GENUS *PSEPHENUS*[3] (WATER PENNY)

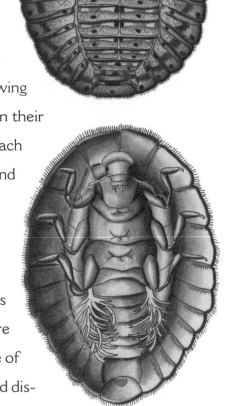

Ecology: Water pennies are flattened because, like some mayflies, they live in fast-flowing water. They use the plates on their backs like a suction cup to attach themselves to rocks or logs, and they feed on algae growing on these substrates.

Cool fact: There are only two genera of water pennies in the United States. They are called water pennies because of their flattened, oval shape and distinctive coppery color.

---

[1] Pronounced: *"KOHL-ee-OOP-ter-uh"*   [3] Pronounced: *"sih-FEE-nus"*
[2] Pronounced: *"sih-FEN-ih-DEE"*

Norris:

PHYLUM NEMATOMORPHA[1]
(HORSEHAIR WORM)

Ecology: Juvenile horsehair worms are parasites, mainly to insects, living inside the host and absorbing dissolved nutrients. As the horsehair worm reaches adulthood, and their host comes into contact with water, it bursts out of the host, killing it in the process. Adults are free-living, but have no digestive system and do not feed. Instead, they live off nutrients they absorbed as juveniles.

Cool fact: Horsehair worms get their name because in the days before cars, when horses were the primary form of transportation, the sudden appearance of these long, slender worms in mud puddles caused people to believe they were hairs from horses' tails that had come to life.

[1] Pronounced: *"nee-MAT-oh-MOR-fuh"*

Harry:

PHYLUM ARTHROPODA

CLASS INSECTA

ORDER EPHEMEROPTERA

FAMILY LEPTOHYPHIDAE[1]

GENUS *TRICORYTHODES* [2] (LITTLE STOUT CRAWLER MAYFLY)

Ecology: *Tricorythodes* mayflies are rock-clinging bottom dwellers in streams. They feed on algae and diatoms growing on the rocks by scraping the rocks with their mandibles[3] (jaws). They are fairly tolerant, which means you can find them in a wide range of habitats, such as cool mountain streams with a closed tree canopy or warmer, open-canopy streams with lots of sunlight.

Cool fact: When juvenile mayflies emerge as adults, they often form swarms of thousands, if not millions of mayflies. Almost all of the swarming mayflies are males. You can tell they are mayflies by their bobbing motion—they fly quickly upward, then spread their wings and float downward, then fly upward again. Since mayfly adults are short-lived, large swarms can leave so many dead mayflies on roads that the pavement becomes slippery and dangerous for cars!

[1] Pronounced: *"lep-toe-HYE-fih-dee"*   [3] Pronounced: *"man-DIH-bullz"*

[2] Pronounced: *"TRY-korr-ee-THOE-deez"*

Old Griswald

PHYLUM TARDIGRADA[1]
(WATER BEAR)

Ecology: Water bears live in water, on mosses, or in moist leaf litter or lichens.[2] They must always be in a film of water to survive, otherwise they undergo cryptobiosis,[3] which is the ability to dehydrate and reduce their metabolic rate to withstand extreme environmental conditions, similar to how real bears hibernate every winter. They feed by piercing plant cells with their stylet and sucking out the juices (like a mosquito!).

Cool fact: Water bears that have undergone cryptobiosis can remain dormant for 30 years or more and still come back to life once they are put back in water.

---

[1] Pronounced: *"tard-ih-GRADE-uh"*   [3] Pronounced: *"KRIPT-oh-bye-OH-sis"*
[2] Pronounced: *"LIKE-enz"*

The Mussel:

Phylum Mollusca[1]
Class Bivalvia[2]
(Freshwater
Mussels)

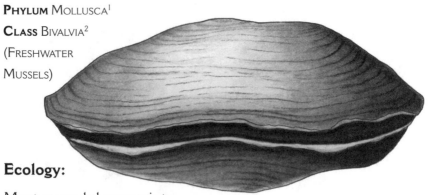

Ecology:

Most mussels burrow into stream sediments and rarely move. They are filter feeders and have cilia[3] (tiny hair-like filaments) to draw water across their gills, where food particles get trapped in a sticky mucous. Because they filter the water, mollusks[4] are important for maintaining good water quality.

Cool fact: Mussels have sticky threads called byssal[5] threads that they secrete to attach themselves to rocks. These threads are very stretchy but also very strong, and scientists have studied these threads to see if they can copy their properties and use them to engineer strong, yet flexible materials.

---

[1] Pronounced: *"moe-LUSK-uh"*
[2] Pronounced: *"bye-VAL-vee-uh"*
[3] Pronounced: *"SILL-ee-uh"*

[4] Pronounced: *"MALL-usks"*
[5] Pronounced: *"BISS-uhl"*

The Midge:

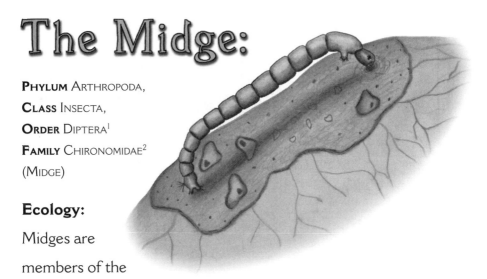

PHYLUM ARTHROPODA,
CLASS INSECTA,
ORDER DIPTERA[1]
FAMILY CHIRONOMIDAE[2]
(MIDGE)

Ecology:

Midges are members of the true flies, which means they only have 1 set of wings (most insects have 2 sets of wings). They are often the most common insect found in streams. Many are herbivores and feed on algae or detritus[3] (dead plants). Midges are a very important part of a fish's diet.

Cool fact: Midges can live in a wide range of conditions, including deep or slow-moving water that may not have a lot of oxygen. In this case, some midges have erythrocruorin,[4] a protein that looks bright red and works like hemoglobin to carry oxygen. These midges are known as 'bloodworms.'

[1] Pronounced: *"DIP-terr-uh"*
[2] Pronounced: *"KYE-row-NO-mid-ee"*
[3] Pronounced: *"dee-TRY-tuss"*
[4] Pronounced: *"ee-REE-throw-KROR-in"*

Callie:

PHYLUM ARTHROPODA
CLASS INSECTA
ORDER TRICHOPTERA[1]
FAMILY HYDROPSYCHIDAE[2]
GENUS *CHEUMATOPSYCHE*[3]
(LITTLE SISTER SEDGE CADDISFLY)

Ecology: Caddisflies like cool, clean water. Many build net-like retreats, which is their home and also a way to capture food particles, sort of like a spider's web. Most caddisflies are worm-like, with a soft abdomen that may have filamentous[4] gills on it.

Cool fact: Some caddisflies build cases to live in instead of nets. These cases are like tiny sleeping bags made out of small stones or pieces of leaves or wood. The caddisflies drag them around on the bottom of the stream and they can retreat inside the case if they sense danger.

---

[1] Pronounced: *"try-COP-terr-uh"*

[2] Pronounced: *"hye-droe-SIGH-kid-dee"*

[3] Pronounced: *"kew-MAT-oh-SIGH-key"*

[4] Pronounced: *"fill-uh-MINT-us"*

Pauli:

PHYLUM ARTHROPODA,
CLASS INSECTA,
ORDER PLECOPTERA[1]
FAMILY PERILIDAE[2]
GENUS *PERLESTA*[3]
(GOLDEN STONE)

Ecology: Juvenile
stonefly nymphs are
long-lived, preferring clean, cool
water. Most feed on dead leaves,
but some are predatory in the
early spring. Stoneflies are
indicators of good water
quality.

Cool fact: Stonefly adults are one of the most popular
fly-fishing flies. Some adult stoneflies emerge very early
in the spring, while there is still snow on the ground. If
you are lucky, you can catch them crawling across the
snow away from a stream.

[1] Pronounced: *"play-COP-terr-uh"*   [3] Pronounced: *"PER-lest-uh"*
[2] Pronounced: *"PER-lid-ee"*

The Dragonfly:

PHYLUM ARTHROPODA
CLASS INSECTA
ORDER ODONATA[1]
SUBORDER ANISOPTERA[2]
(DRAGONFLY)

Ecology: Dragonflies are predators, both as juvenile nymphs and as adults. Some juvenile dragonflies stalk their prey, while others burrow into sediments and surprise attack their prey. They are common inhabitants of shallow, slow-moving streams, marshes, and ponds.

Cool fact: Juvenile dragonflies are predatory and eat just about anything smaller than them, including aquatic insects like mayflies or midges and even small fish! Adult dragonflies eat lots of mosquitoes, so it's good to have dragonflies around.

[1] Pronounced: *"OH-den-NOT-uh"*   [2] Pronounced: *AN-iss-OPP-ter-uh"*

Meet the Illustrators

Rachel Renne lives in Missoula, Montana, but grew up exploring the forests and creeks of southwest Florida while serving as official bug ambassador for her three sisters. On hot days, they would spend hours in the creek behind their house, digging alien-looking creatures out of the mud. In college, Rachel studied entomology and fit as many bugs as she could into the illustrations for a book about the Charlotte Harbor Watershed. It was a thrill to co-illustrate Seth and Mattie's Big River Adventure, where invertebrates are the stars! You can contact Rachel at racheopod@gmail.com.

Although **Heidi Anderson** spent much of her childhood catching tadpoles and tromping around the lush creeks of Western Oregon, it took many years and several college degrees for her to fully appreciate the incredible diversity of life that lies, often unseen, just beneath the water's surface. She is excited to be part of a project that combines her passions for drawing and stream ecology, and that brings the hidden world of freshwater insects to life. These days, she can be found floating, hiking, and working in and around the streams and rivers of Western Montana. Contact her at heidieliseanderson@gmail.com

Terri Moore lives in Dardanelle, Arkansas. She has been happily married since 2001 and has four amazing children, three dogs, and one cat. She loves hiking, mountain biking, remodeling houses, reading, and all things art. She is thankful for all the blessings in her life and is astounded by God's goodness on a daily basis. Contact Terri at olds67moore@gmail.com.